SMALL TOWN GHOSTS

KEVIN JOHNSON

SMALL TOWN
GHOSTS

COPYRIGHT

FOREWORD

The following is a modern-day fairy tale inspired by the small town where I grew up. A few pieces of the story were influenced by events from my childhood, a few by events from my adulthood, but mostly it's a fabrication.

In my mind, many — but not all — of the actors playing the characters within are people I know, or know of, but that doesn't mean they are the same as the part they play. It just means I see them as movie stars playing a role. Anything more than general similarities is unintentional.

Also in my mind, the locations are — or sometimes were — real places, though I have changed the names and taken great liberties with most. If you're from there, maybe you will recognize a few. Most importantly, the story is fiction. Keep that in mind and don't go looking for buried treasure.

Mike liked the smell of the grocery store at night. Although, if he stopped to think about it, maybe it wasn't the smell but more the fact that it was still and quiet, with only the occasional shopper passing by, offering a smile or a nod.

And maybe quiet wasn't the right word. Music played from somewhere overhead, bouncing off every harshly lit surface, while refrigeration units hummed in unison. But it was a kind of quiet, the sort where there was no chatter, no activity, no getting stuck in a conversation with someone he barely knew. Occasionally, a song would catch his attention, evoke an old memory, but mostly it was just background noise.

And maybe night wasn't the right word, either. The

time was just after 8pm, but it was the heart of summer and daylight would be clinging to the small town until a few minutes after nine. Even if Mike stayed until the store closed, he would still be home before dark.

And home *definitely* wasn't the right word. It was a house and that was all.

Whatever the case, he needed bread, so he pulled a loaf from the shelf. There was meaning in the color of the twist tie, one he couldn't recall for certain, but he thought it indicated the day the bread was baked, and therefore, how fresh it would be. Lacking the details, he went with the tried-and-true method of giving it a squeeze, then dropped it into the handbasket that was hooked over his left arm.

He always used the handbasket. His frequent trips in for a few items at a time eliminated the need for a cart. There was, of course, the added bonus that the handbasket never had a bad wheel, never sent him struggling through the store while people stared as he went clacking by, trying to hold a straight line.

Carts were the worst.

On the same aisle, he grabbed a jar of extra chunky peanut butter and wandered to the dairy section for a gallon of milk. Next stop was the cereal aisle, where he faced his toughest decision of the day. Cocoa Pebbles, or something grown-up?

He left the aisle with the largest box of Cocoa Pebbles available.

At the checkout, it was business as usual. A single lane

was open, manned by the same bored-looking mono-tone teenage girl that was there most evenings. The only difference was a surprisingly long line of two people. For the hour, it was a sizable crowd.

As he joined the line, the woman in front of him turned to grab a tube of ChapStick from the impulse rack. He recognized her immediately and almost dropped his groceries.

When she glanced at him, he smiled and nodded. She returned the gesture.

As long as it had been and as unexpected as it was, there was no denying who he was seeing. His first in-stinct was to remain quiet, let the moment pass by and disappear forever.

Sadly, he had never been good at following his in-stincts. And besides, there was no way she would re-member him.

He took a deep breath and said, "Excuse me."

The woman half-turned.

"Hi," he said, "aren't you Kayla Warner?"

She half-smiled and nodded. "I am."

"I thought so. We went to high school together."

She studied his face, trying to place him.

"I'm sure you won't remember me," he added. "I was a few years behind you. Two, actually. We didn't know each other."

The person in line ahead of them, an older lady, paused as she was paying for her groceries, eyed them, and went back to counting out coins to match the total of her purchase.

"You must have a good memory," Kayla said. "I'm not certain I can recall everyone from my own class, small as it was, let alone any others."

She seemed friendly enough, considering she was being chatted up in line at the grocery store.

"It comes and goes," Mike said.

The lady in front of them finished paying and walked away, followed by the bag boy pushing her cart jammed full of groceries.

"Did you find everything all right?" Monotone Checkout Girl asked as she lowered the front gate of Kayla's cart and began scanning items.

"Yes, thank you," Kayla replied, then turned back to Mike. "Do you still live here in town?"

"Recently moved back. Temporarily." He winced. Adding that one word changed everything, made it sound like he had fallen on hard times and had returned home to regroup, get his life in order.

The fact that it was true made it worse.

"What about you?" he asked, though he knew the answer. She had disappeared after graduation, off to whatever the world held for her. He hadn't seen her since.

"I'm just in town for a short while."

"Visiting family and friends?"

She shook her head. "My mom passed away."

"Oh. I'm sorry to hear that."

She smiled a warm and sad smile and said, "Thanks."

"That'll be 71.67," Monotone Checkout Girl said.

Kayla dug in her purse, pulled out cash and handed it over.

The voice in Mike's head told him to stop where he was and let the conversation wrap up, but he couldn't help himself.

"Do you mind if ask when the funeral is?"

"It was three weeks ago. This is my second trip back to go through her things and figure out what to do with the house."

"I see. Well, I'm truly sorry to hear that. It must be tough."

She nodded as she held out her hand for her change, then dropped the money into her purse.

"Nice meeting you," she said.

"You, too. Good luck with everything."

"Thanks." She turned and walked away, pushing her cart because the bag boy had yet to return. Mike watched her go for a moment, awed by what just happened. Not in a thousand years could he have imagined their paths crossing again. And yet, there she went. She had changed so little that he could practically see the homecoming queen crown still on her head.

"Hi, Mr. Ellerton. Did you find everything all right?" Monotone Checkout Girl asked.

Mike sat his handbasket on the conveyer. "You have to stop calling me that."

"Sure thing, Mr. Ellerton," she replied, her tone un-wavering.

"It makes me sound old, which I'm not."

She stopped what she was doing and stared at him, face blank, for three full seconds, then resumed scanning.

Mike sighed. "So, how's class going?"

"Fine. I've got a test tomorrow. I hate algebra."

"You and me both."

"You've got a test tomorrow, too?"

"No, I meant I hate —" He realized she was messing with him. "Never mind."

After his items were rung up and paid for, he walked out into the warm evening air. A silver SUV sat one spot over from his Jeep, the back hatch raised. The rest of the lot was empty.

As he approached, the hatch closed and Kayla pushed her empty basket into view. They glanced at each other and nodded as she passed by.

As Mike unlocked his own door and dropped the single bag onto the passenger seat, he heard a noise. When he looked back, Kayla was struggling to get the front wheels of the cart up on the curb.

"I got it," he said, jogging over and lifting the cart onto the sidewalk. "I'll take it in."

She smiled and let go. "Thank you."

"No worries," he said. "Have a good evening." He guided the cart back into the store, docking it with the rest. When he came out, he was surprised to see her still there. He was more surprised when she took a step toward him.

"Hey, do you happen to know a good place to grab a bite to eat at this hour?"

Mike glanced at his watch. 8:39.

"I do," he said. "Cane's is open until ten tonight, if you like barbecue."

The late day light glowed gold around her, and Mike had to remind himself not to stare.

"I think I've seen that. Isn't it across from where the radio station used to be?"

The radio station. Mike had forgotten about that. He smiled at the memory. "KJON, 93 point... something," he said.

"Five, maybe?" She tilted her head as she tried to recall. "It's been so long, I can't remember."

"Me either. But, you're right. That's where it's at."

"Sounds good. I've been eating too much fast food lately. Thanks for the recommendation."

"You're welcome. And you won't be disappointed, I promise."

"I'm sure I won't. Thanks again." She turned to leave but stopped. "Hey, I know this sounds a little strange, but would you like to join me?"

Holy crap, he thought.

"If you're not busy," she added.

He tried his best to remain calm. "I'm not busy at all."

"Great. I always feel awkward sitting in a restaurant alone."

"Understandable."

"Shall we meet there in, say, 20 minutes? Is that enough time?"

"Works for me."

"Okay. See you then."

She climbed into her SUV while Mike managed to get into his Jeep without soiling himself. He waited until she was gone before moving.

The house had been built at some point in the '30s. It had since been renovated, but even that had taken place decades earlier. For all its lack of modern design, Mike had to admit it carried a certain charm in the daylight. With its high ceilings and real wood floors that were scuffed and worn, and its ornate banister and staircase railing that wobbled as the stairs creaked, it had what people called character.

He was sold on it right away, but that had more to do with the low rent and it being the only worthwhile place in town. Everything else available had been a step down. A large step. And the location was good. It sat tucked away behind the courthouse in the center of town, just off the main road, on the edge of an older neighborhood that wasn't fancy but was clean and quiet.

If he had toured the place when dark, he might not have been so quick to move in. The charm had disappeared after sundown. The first thing he had noticed was the lighting. The old fixtures and low wattage bulbs were nowhere near adequate, leaving the many nooks and crannies dark with shadows that always seemed to be moving. He knew it was in his head, just a figment of his imagination, but it was unsettling nonetheless.

And that wasn't the worst of it. The worst was the creaking. Throughout the night, the house would groan and sigh. At times, a series of creaks would occur that gave Mike the impression of someone walking across the floor. And it was always coming from somewhere in the house that he wasn't. When he was downstairs, the sounds would come from upstairs and vice versa. Or it would come from another room. There was never a good clear creaking where he happened to be, unless he was moving, in which case there was plenty.

Early on, the nights had freaked him out to the point that he slept very little and had left a light on. He kept telling himself to quit being ridiculous, that all old houses made noises, but it didn't help. He had spent the previous 15 years in a house that he and his ex-wife had built that never made a sound, so he wasn't used to the cacophony. Several weeks passed before he slept with the lights off, and that only after he had picked up a cheap nightlight at the dollar store and plugged it in across the room. There were nights he would still leave the hallway light on, but mostly he was getting accustomed to the place and its creepiness. Mostly.

After putting away the groceries, he stood in the

kitchen, leaning against the counter. The drive from the store to the house was barely two minutes, and putting away the few items he had bought killed three more. Five down, fifteen to go.

For a moment, he felt strange. Something was off. He realized this was the first time in a long while that he was looking forward to something. He had been walking through each day numb for so long, he could scarcely recall having ever felt the sensation at all.

Five minutes later, he gave up waiting and left.

A haze of smoke hung in the air inside Cane's. It was always there, not thick, but enough to notice. It came in through the backdoor, blowing in from the smoker that sat behind the restaurant.

Mike had eaten there plenty since moving back. It was the only place in town open past nine and, like the grocery store, it kept him distracted at the time of day when things went from bad to worse.

The waiting area was small with only a handful of seats. One of those seats, pulled over into the corner by itself, was taken by an older gentleman, bent over an electric guitar, playing blues riffs, and lost in a world only he was seeing. He was a fixture there, mostly on week-ends, but sometimes showing up on a random week-night. When he sat down and slowly removed his guitar from its case and plugged it in, the staff would turn off the music that was broadcast in his stead. He would test the strings, the volume, the tuning, then would sink into the chair and start playing. He never played anything loud or fast. It was always clean and slow, a melancholy type of blues that filled the room all the way up to the high ceilings with a certain aura that was hard to place. Whatever it was, Mike wallowed in it.

Cane's was in one of a row of buildings in the old downtown, built sometime near the turn of the century. It had been a clothing store long ago, then stood empty for years before Cane's moved in, remodeling the old structure and breathing new life into it, but the old charm remained.

The front door, glass and wood and painted a deep, rich, red, opened. Mike glanced up from the floor, pulling his focus from the notes as Kayla stepped into the room. Her white dress, the same she had been wearing in the grocery store, contrasted with her tanned skin in a way that made it hard not to stare. The dress was somewhere between the playful, summer dress of a young girl, and the elegant sophistication of a woman. It wasn't just the dress that seemed to straddle a line between two contrasting worlds, it was everything about her. Her hair, her smile, the way she carried herself. In all of those things, Mike swore he could see the uncertainty of youth and the confidence of age, swirling together.

He stood and waved.

"I hope I didn't keep you waiting long," she said.

He shook his head and thought it best not to tell her he would have gladly waited the entire night. "I just got here a few minutes ago."

The hostess, a young, dark-haired girl named Lindsay, appeared from the dining room. "Two?" she asked Mike, a hint of surprise on her face.

"Yes, please."

She grabbed two menus and two bundles of silverware from behind a small counter. "Right this way."

Mike gestured for Kayla to go ahead of him. He made a point of not staring as he followed.

The dining room was a large, open space that sat between the waiting area and the kitchen. Only two tables were occupied, one by a younger couple, and one by a family with two kids. It seemed late to have the kids out eating, but who was Mike to criticize.

Lindsay led them to a small table for two halfway back and along the wall.

"What can I get you to drink?" she asked Kayla.

"I'll have water."

She looked at Mike. "The usual?"

"Yes, please," he said with a smile.

She laid the menus on the table. "Be right back."

"The usual?" Kayla asked. "I take it you come here often."

"Way more than I should."

Though he had every dish memorized and already knew what he wanted, Mike picked up a menu and opened it, studying the pages without seeing anything on them as he tried to process what was happening to him.

"How often do you make it back here to visit?" he asked.

"Not often. When I came in for the funeral, it was the first time I had been here in almost ten years."

"Wow. Why so long?"

She picked up the remaining menu and ignored his question. "So, what's good?"

Mike took the hint, filed it away.

"Everything. And I'm not just saying that. I think I've been through the entire menu in the last few months."

"The last few months? You weren't kidding when you said you come here more than you should." She scanned the menu a moment longer before laying it aside. "At the grocery store, you said you had recently moved back. How long ago was that?"

Mike tried counting backwards in his head, but the days had been blurring together for a while now. Time was becoming an abstract idea, something he could no longer measure with any accuracy.

"Four months, maybe."

"How long were you gone?" she asked.

"Let's see. I left two years into college. So, 21 years."

Mike didn't ask her the same question; he knew she had disappeared shortly after graduation. Instead, he searched for something else, something to keep the conversation going and avoid any awkward pauses.

"Where do you live these days? If you don't mind me asking."

"Indianapolis. We've been there about six years now."

"We?" he asked, despite knowing the answer. He had already noticed the ring on her finger.

She nodded. "Me and my husband. Before that, we were in Idaho, and before that, Colorado. He worked in sales for a large corporation, so we moved a lot. About six years ago, he took a management position, which is what sent us to Indy."

Their waiter, a young man who was a fixture on the closing shift, arrived with their drinks.

"Hey, Mr. Ellerton." He sat the drinks in front of them, not having to ask which was Mike's.

"How's it going, Carson?"

"Good." He pulled a pad and pen from his back pocket. "Are you ready to order, or would you like a little more time?" He looked at Kayla as he asked.

Mike always knew what he wanted right off, and Carson had picked up on that fact months ago and began asking for his order straight away. He was a sharp kid.

Because Mike visited Cane's almost as often as the grocery store, he knew that Carson, and Monotone Checkout Girl for that matter, had just graduated from the local high school and was preparing for college in the fall. While Monotone Checkout Girl was getting a head start by taking summer courses at a small college a few towns over, Carson was picking up as many shifts as he could, practically working full-time, to save money before heading out of state.

"I think I'll have the smoked chicken," Kayla said.

"Very well. And for you, Mr. Ellerton?"

Like Monotone Checkout Girl, Carson always referred to Mike as Mr. Ellerton. Mike had given up trying to dissuade him from doing so. The kid was just too polite to do anything else, whereas Monotone Checkout Girl did it solely to annoy him. He wished he had never paid with a credit card so she wouldn't know his name. She'd probably call him sir, though. That was just as bad.

After Mike gave his order, Carson thanked them, gathered the menus, and ran off to the kitchen.

Kayla let her gaze wander around the room, took in the decorations, the high ceilings, the hardwood floors. "You said you were a few years behind me in school?"

Mike nodded as she refocused and studied his face again. He looked away, pretended to watch the old man working at the strings on his guitar.

"I can't place you," she said. "Sorry."

"That's to be expected, no need to apologize." He turned back to her, propped his elbows on the table. "So, tell me all about Indianapolis. What do you do there?"

She followed his lead, propping her elbows on the table as well, and leaned forward, her posture perfect. "I'm a teacher. Sixth grade English."

"Sixth grade English. Wow. I could use your help. My English is somewhere around the fourth-grade level."

She grinned. "What about you? What do you do?"

"I'm a software developer."

"Sounds exciting."

"I think you misheard me. I'm a software developer."

Kayla grinned, picking up on the joke. "Ah, I see. Sounds terrible."

As they left the restaurant, Mike held the door, catching a hint of her perfume as she glided by. Outside, the night air was cool and the passing traffic was light. Kayla stopped and looked across the road to the storefront that was once the radio station, her face aglow in the soft light of the streetlamp.

"It looks so different from what I remember."

"Yeah," Mike said. "A while back, the outside was remodeled. I forget what was there when it happened, but the radio station was already gone."

"Did you ever listen to it?"

"Just the out-of-town games. You?"

She shook her head. "I didn't like country music."

"Same here."

She stared a moment longer, lost in something Mike assumed was a good memory, then pointed. "I'm down this way."

Several spots down, her silver SUV was parked parallel behind his Jeep.

"Thanks for meeting me," she said as they walked. "That was much better than eating fast food alone in an empty house."

Mike laughed. "That's a pretty low bar, but I'm glad I could help."

She looked again at the missing radio station. "Things have changed so much since high school."

Mike picked up on something in her voice, something wistful. Over 20 years gone, and 10 since the last visit, had to leave a person nostalgic. He wanted to know why she had stayed away, why she hadn't visited in so long, despite having had at least one family member in town.

"Thanks again for buying," she said, smiling. Her teeth were perfect and white, complimented by a subdued red lipstick. "You really didn't have to."

"No worries. In fact, I should be thanking you. This is the first time I haven't eaten alone in a while. I think the staff was thrown a little."

"I picked up on that," she said with a laugh.

Mike realized that telling her that fact didn't reflect well on him.

"How long are you in town?" he asked, changing the subject.

"I'm not certain. Another week or so, maybe. It depends on how things go at mom's house. I have a lot of packing to do." She dug through her purse, pulled out her keys and clicked the remote. The lights on the SUV flashed and the doors clicked.

"Well, good luck," he said. "Do you have anyone helping you? Other family in the area?"

She shook her head. "Mom was the last one."

There was pain hidden in her tone and her expression. She masked it well, but Mike could see it.

"I'm sorry to hear that."

"Thank you."

"If you need help, I'd be more than happy to pitch in however I can."

She didn't answer right away, only watched a passing car as it turned through the stoplight a block down. Mike worried he had overstepped, but he forged ahead.

"I realize that just sounds like an empty platitude," he added, "since we don't know each other. But I'm serious, If you need help, I've got the time. My schedule is flexible. Probably have the energy as well, who knows." He shrugged and grinned.

When she grinned back, he felt a small sense of relief.

"I appreciate the offer, but I can handle it."

"I've no doubt you can. Hey, do you happen to have a pen?"

"I think so," she said, digging into her purse and coming out with one.

Mike pulled the receipt from his pocket and wrote his number on it, handed it and the pen to her.

"If you change your mind, give me a call. I'd be more than happy to help out."

She smiled, stuffed the pen and receipt into her purse. "Thank you. I really appreciate the offer."

"You're welcome." He took a step back, toward his Jeep. "If I don't see you again, good luck with everything and have a safe trip back to Indy."

She smiled and waved as he turned away, climbed into his Jeep, and left.

Back at the house, Mike sat in the Jeep a moment, processing the evening. As they had eaten, he had asked her questions about her job, about her travels since graduation, which place she liked living the most. When she spoke of Indianapolis, there was something in the tone of her voice, the way she wouldn't meet his eye. He had changed the subject, almost asked about high school, but quickly caught himself. They talked about the food, their work, how long the drive from Indy had been. Nothing of importance. It was surreal, after all these years, to be talking to her, having dinner with her, for crying out loud. It was funny how the universe worked sometimes. Well, funny and crappy.

Pulling the keys from the ignition, he climbed out. The lights in the house were on, just as he had left them.

Inside, he sat on the couch, flipped on the TV and turned the volume low. He didn't expect her to call him, and that was probably for the best. Like everything else in his life, it would just end up turning to crap anyway. Best to leave it all in the past.

Around him, the house creaked and groaned.

The next morning, Mike stared at the walls, his laptop sitting idle beside him. He had work to do, which was a rarity as of late, but he couldn't find the motivation to do it. Yesterday had come out of the blue, smacked him in the face, making it hard to concentrate. Common sense told him it was an anomaly, a once in a great while thing. He would return to his routine, Kayla would return to her life elsewhere, and that would be that. Just like high school, their paths would briefly intersect, then diverge. At least this time, she was aware of it. And it hadn't been the disaster it had been back then.

At lunchtime, he gave up altogether and left, drove the four blocks to the library and went inside, the cool air washing over him the moment he walked through the doors. That was another thing about the house. Though the central heat and air unit wasn't ancient, it did struggle to keep the house cool. Maybe it was too small for the space, or maybe it was the fact the house was far from airtight. Whatever the case, it would slowly warm over the course of the day, the air running non-stop. Once the sun went down, it would catch up somewhere in the night and kick off, leaving nothing to mute the creaks and groans.

He greeted the ladies at the circulation desk and exchanged brief pleasantries. Behind them, through a plate glass window, Audrey sat in her office, staring at her computer monitor. Without asking or knocking, Mike entered and sat down in the padded chair in front of her desk.

"I'm glad you're here," she said. "I've got a computer problem."

"Have you tried rebooting?"

She stopped what she was doing long enough to give him a look. "Not that kind of problem." She turned the monitor so he could see it. "The region is buying us some new computers and I don't know what I should get. Which of these do you think would be good?"

Mike studied the screen, scanning the specs of the options she had pulled up, then pointed to the one he thought was best for the price. "That one."

"That one it is," she said, repositioning the monitor. "So, what are you up to today?"

Her question was more than idle chitchat, though she always tried to mask it for his sake.

"Just taking a short break. I had a small project come in."

"That's great," she said, her face lighting up.

"Yeah. Hey, any news on the regional director position?"

Her excitement increased to the point Mike thought her head might split open. She bounced up and down in her chair and clasped her hands together. "Anne called this morning. She wants to meet with me next week. She didn't say what it was about, but I've got a good feeling."

"You know you've got it."

She shushed him, gave a stern look. "I don't want to jinx it."

"Don't worry," he said, laughing. "How could they possibly choose anyone else?"

"Oh, they could easily choose someone else. There are four good candidates within the region alone, never mind the outside applicants."

Mike waved a dismissive hand. "Doesn't matter. They know you and they know what you've done with this branch."

"Yeah, but still..."

Mike could see the doubt in her expression.

"Alright, look. I'll drive down and talk to them. Put in a good word, do a little schmoozing. Turn on the ol' charm. By the time I'm finished, they'll be begging you to take the job."

"You have charm?" Audrey asked, her expression serious. "You've done a fantastic job of hiding it all these years."

"That's the other thing I have: a great poker face. That's why you didn't know I was full of charm."

She made a sound somewhere between a grunt and a laugh and rolled her eyes. "You're definitely full of something. I'm not sure it's charm."

Mike laced his fingers across his stomach and relaxed back into the chair. "Charm, charm, charm. Hey, what's that thing where you say a word so many times it loses its meaning?"

"Semantic satiation."

"I think that's happening to me right now with the word charm," Mike said. "And see, the fact that you know that off the top of your head means you know all kinds of things. And that's why they'll pick you."

"Did you just come here to annoy me or is there something I can help you with?" she asked.

"To annoy you."

"Well, mission accomplished."

When Mike returned to the house, he went straight to work, but found himself distracted by Audrey's potential promotion. He was proud of his friend, that much was certain. For as long as he had known her, which was as far back as he could remember, she had loved books. Growing up, her bedroom in her parents' house, which had been two blocks from his own, had books scattered on the floor more often than not. Even the treehouse in their backyard had a small, makeshift bookcase filled with mystery-solving characters from Encyclopedia Brown to the Hardy Boys. They had spent many of their childhood days in that treehouse, reading silently side by side, then comparing notes, guessing the culprits. She had been right more than he had. Much more. That she had become a librarian and risen in the ranks was no surprise. Still, he worried what would happen if she got the job.

Around five, Mike stopped work for the day. Eyeing the clock, he settled into the couch for a long evening and wondered what items he might need from the grocery store. Or maybe there was something he needed from the dollar store. Anything to get out of the house for a bit.

His phone rang and he picked it up from the coffee table, checked the screen and saw a number from an area code he didn't recognize. Had to be a telemarketer, or more accurately, an automated voice trying to sell him something. He couldn't recall the last time an actual living, breathing, telemarketer had called. The poor souls — they had been rendered obsolete by robots, victims of technology like so many others.

The call went to voicemail as he tossed the phone back onto the table and sunk into the cushions, continued searching for reasons to get out for a while.

The phone dinged, indicating a text message. The notification showed the same number that had just called and Mike realized who it probably was.

"Crap," he said out loud, opening the message.

Hey, this is Kayla. I just tried calling but got your voicemail… thought I would text in case you thought I was a telemarketer. If the offer for help still stands, I've changed my mind. I could use a hand.

He hit the call button and she answered on the second ring.

"Hi."

"Hey. I am so sorry I didn't answer your call. You were right, I thought you were a telemarketer."

"No problem," she said through a small laugh. "I think everyone is conditioned to ignore calls from outside their area code."

"True. I usually ignore most from inside it as well."

"Same here. I hope I'm not interrupting your evening."

"Not at all," Mike assured her. "How's it going with your mom's things?"

He heard a sigh on her end of the line. "I'm starting to get worried there's more here than I can handle before I have to go back to Indianapolis. Does your offer to help still stand?"

"Of course. I can come over now if you would like."

"Are you sure? I don't want to impose on such short notice."

"Of course I'm sure," Mike said. "I'm more than happy to help however I can."

"Okay. I'll text you the address. And thank you."

"No problem. See you in a few minutes."

Mike hung up, grabbed his keys and headed for the front door, but paused when he realized his wallet was upstairs on the nightstand. He bounded up the creaking stairs, holding his breath that they wouldn't collapse beneath him. In the bedroom, he flipped on the light, stuffed his wallet in his pocket and left, leaving the light on.

On his way down the stairs, Kayla's message with her address came through. He recognized the street but checked the maps app to make sure he knew exactly where the house was.

Satisfied and nervous, he locked the door as he left, then made the short drive across town.

The house was in a nice neighborhood that sat along a low ridge behind the high school. He recognized her SUV, parked behind it, and climbed out. Before he reached the porch, Kayla opened the door and stepped out.

For a brief moment, Mike thought he had slipped back in time. In jeans and a t-shirt, her hair pulled back in a ponytail, it was high school all over again.

"Thank you for coming," she said, stepping aside to let him in.

Mike surveyed the living room and what he could see of the kitchen. Boxes were strewn about, lids open, some full, some empty. Stacks of plates sat on the kitchen counter, and shelves still held the knickknacks that had likely been in place for decades. Framed pictures dotted the walls.

"It's a good thing you called," he said.

"I really appreciate your help," Kayla said as she sank onto the end of the couch. She blew a strand of hair out of her eyes and leaned her head back.

Mike sat on the other end and took in the room. It was dark out, just past 10pm. In the four hours they had been working, they had accomplished a great deal.

"We really put a dent in it, didn't we?"

"Much more than I thought we could."

He was about to compliment her on her hard work when she stood, disappeared into the kitchen and returned with two bottles of water.

"I think we earned these."

Mike took one, unscrewed the top and held it up. "To your mom. From what I've seen here, she was a woman of fine taste."

Kayla smiled and tapped her bottle against his. "To Mom."

They drank, Mike draining a quarter of the bottle before coming up for air.

"Any idea what you're going to do with the place?"

Kayla pursed her lips, gave her head the slightest of shakes.

"I'm not sure."

An idea had occurred to Mike earlier in the evening,

but he hadn't broached the subject. Maybe now was a good time.

"Have you considered renting it out?"

"Not really. Why? Do you know someone who's looking?"

"I could use a new place," he said. "The house I'm in is sort of driving me crazy."

Kayla grinned. "How so?"

Mike shrugged as he surveyed the room again. "It's mostly old-house problems." He didn't want to elaborate, to tell her the house creeped him out to the point of sleeping with a nightlight. "I've looked at everything in town and there's just nothing good. This is a nice place. It would be a big improvement. If you wanted to keep it simple, I could pay you direct, keep maintenance done on the place for you until I figure out what I'm doing long-term. And if you decided you wanted to sell at any point, I'd be fine with clearing out. I wouldn't hold you to anything." He looked over at her. "No pressure, though. It was just a thought I had. I realize you hardly know me and it might be a little crazy to trust me with your mother's home while you're hundreds of miles away."

Kayla stood and crossed the room, looked out the front window. After a moment she turned, crossed her arms, and leaned against the sill. "To tell you the truth, I *have* been considering keeping it a while, though renting it out hadn't crossed my mind."

Mike didn't want to get his hopes up, but he was

liking what he was hearing. If she wanted to keep the house around, surely she would like the idea of making some dough off it. He stood and stretched, placing his hands on his lower back which had started aching hours ago. Not wanting to push his luck, he decided to drop the subject while he was ahead. The seed had been planted, that was good enough for now.

"Anything else you want to get accomplished before we call it a night?"

"I think we've done plenty," she said. "This gives me a good head start on the rest." Her eyes passed over the stack of boxes, labeled and closed, the shelves and kitchen counter now empty. "I can't thank you enough for your help. Really."

"My pleasure. If you want, I can drop by tomorrow and give you a hand again."

She uncrossed her arms and stood up from the sill. "I hate to take up another one of your evenings."

Mike waved a dismissive hand. "No worries. I've got some work I need to do in the morning, but I'll be done by lunch. I can come by around noon, get an early start. Besides, I would appreciate the distraction."

She nodded and looked down at the floor. Mike had the feeling she wanted to say something, but she remained quiet.

"Is everything okay?" he asked, then realized he might be overstepping his bounds. Maybe she preferred not to hurry through her mother's things. Maybe she needed to take it slow, come to terms with her loss. "Oh hey, look, if I'm out of line, just let me know and I'll leave you be. I promise I won't take it personally. I understand if you need to take it slow or need time alone here. And that whole thing about me renting from you, you can ignore me. It was just wishful thinking —"

"Oh, no," she interrupted. "It's not that. I was just thinking. And honestly, the sooner I can get through everything, the better. I would greatly appreciate some more help."

Mike hoped she wasn't simply being polite, but best as he could tell, she was sincere. Not that he was any good at reading what others were thinking. If he had been, he might still be married. Or, more likely, divorced long before now.

"Are you sure?" he asked.

She nodded. "Yes, I'm sure."

"Then it's settled." He clapped his hands together. "How about I pick up a pizza on my way over? What do you like?"

"Anything with thick crust," she said.

"Get out of here. You're a thick crust person?"

She grinned and nodded. "You?"

"Of course," he said. "If you ask me, there are two choices in this world that determine the quality of an individual." He held up a finger. "Their choice in pizza crust." He raised a second finger. "And their choice in peanut butter. Thick versus thin, smooth versus chunky. It tells me everything I need to know about a person."

She looked at him sideways, her grin widening. "*That* tells you everything you need to know about a person?"

"Of course. Don't you have some sort of indicator, something you measure people against, so you know what type of person they are?"

"I usually just, you know, ask them questions until I get to know them."

"Different strokes, I guess," Mike said, grinning.

"I guess."

Despite how tired he was, Mike still found her smile captivating, but the mental exhaustion of keeping himself from staring was wearing on him. She was, after all, a married woman, not that it really mattered. There wasn't a chance that his high school dreams would be coming true; he understood that. He wasn't completely delusional. Still, he found himself drifting off course at times and quickly had to correct.

He moved toward the door and Kayla followed him out onto the porch. Bugs of various sizes, mostly small, circled the porch light in a frenzy. She followed him to his Jeep, where he stopped to say goodnight.

"See you tomorrow around noon?"

She nodded. "I'll be here."

"Have a good night."

She stood where she was, next to the drive, as he pulled away.

A few minutes later, he turned into his own driveway, shut off the engine and the headlights. Each window of the house glowed with the dim light of the underpowered bulbs inside, save one. The upstairs bedroom. He must have forgotten to leave it on.

----

26 Years Earlier

Mike pulled at the tie around his neck and tried to hide behind his friends. Why did he have to wear a tie? No one else was wearing one. The girls were all wearing dresses, ranging from casual to formal. The guys mostly wore jeans and t-shirts, with the occasional button-down shirt, but he was the only guy with a tie. For someone who wanted nothing more than to blend into the background, it was a questionable move.

"So, what are we going to do?" Dave asked, yelling to be heard over the music. "Just stand here?"

"I'm fine with that," Graham said. "I told you guys I don't know how to dance."

Dave rolled his eyes. "Come on. The whole point of coming to a dance is to dance. With girls." He smacked Mike on the shoulder. "Are you in?"

Mike looked out at the gym floor, his anxiety level rising. "I don't know," he said.

"What?" Dave yelled.

"I don't know," Mike said, louder.

"Oh come on. Am I the only one with enough nerve to go ask someone to dance?"

Mike and Graham looked at each, then at Dave, and nodded.

"You guys are such losers. Come on."

"I'm not a loser," Graham said.

"Are too."

"Am not."

As the two argued back and forth, Mike scanned the crowd, stopping when he saw her. Everything else faded away, the music, the lights, the other students, everything. He watched her as she laughed and talked to her group of friends, the homecoming queen crown on her head.

As far as Mike was concerned, Kayla was the most incredible creature he had ever seen. Her delicate features and high cheekbones, long brown hair and tanned skin, all wove together into a tapestry of exquisite beauty. In addition to being voted homecoming queen, she was the captain of the cheerleading squad and the most popular girl in school. She only hung out with the most popular kids. On top of all that, she was dating a football player.

Trevor.

Mike and his friends had been lucky. They had yet to be targeted by Trevor and his cronies, but Mike had witnessed others who had, and it wasn't pretty.

"So, what do you say?" Dave said, pulling Mike's attention back.

"To what?"

"Were you not listening? Go ask Audrey to dance. She's over there with her friends. Now is the perfect time."

Growing up, he and Audrey had spent countless hours reading books, riding their bikes as fast as they could make them go, laughing and yelling over boardgames and TV shows, and playing tag under the streetlights until their parents called them in. Though they were close friends, asking her to dance would be awkward.

"I don't know," he said. "I don't think that's a good idea."

"Why not?" Dave asked.

Mike shrugged. "I don't know. I just — I don't know."

Dave rolled his eyes. "You two are hopeless. I'm going to go ask her myself." He spun and walked off.

"Tell me again why we came here?" Graham asked.

Mike looked across the dance floor, spotted Kayla again. "Good question," he said. After a moment, he managed to take his eyes off her and search for Dave, surprised to see him actually leading Audrey onto the dance floor.

He leaned in close, so Graham could hear him. "I'm going to hit the bathroom. Be right back."

"Don't leave me standing here alone like some dork." Graham said. "I'm coming too."

They threaded their way through small clusters of their fellow students to the west end of the gym. A narrow corridor ran beside the bleachers, leading to the lobby. Halfway down the corridor was the men's room. Mike breathed a small sigh of relief as he pushed the door open and saw the room was empty. He didn't like using public restrooms, especially at school. He went into the first stall and closed the door as Graham chose one at the opposite end.

When he was finished, Mike flushed and exited the stall, going to the sinks to wash his hands. As he was squirting soap from the dispenser into his palm, the bathroom door opened. He glanced up at the mirror in front of him and saw Trevor, Robbie and Lance walking in.

Mike quickly lowered his gaze back to his hands.

"Hey Trevor, isn't that the guy that was eyeing your woman?"

"I do believe you're right."

Mike panicked. Graham was still in the stall and no one else was in the bathroom with them, yet Mike tried to convince himself that Robbie wasn't talking about him. Someone else must have come in, some poor soul who was now a hapless target.

He swallowed hard and looked in the mirror again. The three of them were standing behind him. His eyes locked on Trevor.

"Were you staring at my girl?" Trevor asked.

Mike didn't move an inch.

Trevor turned to Lance. "Was this guy staring at my girl?"

"He was staring alright."

"Turn around, nerd," Trevor said. "Before I turn you around myself."

Mike's hands were still wet, but he did as he was told. He dropped his eyes to his feet.

"Look at me when I'm talking to you, nerd," Trevor said.

Mike could hear amusement and meanness mixing

in Trevor's voice. It was a dangerous combination. He kept staring at his shoes.

"You ask me," Robbie said, "I think he's scared."

"Is that so? You scared, nerd?"

Somewhere, he wasn't sure where, Mike found the nerve to raise his eyes to meet Trevor's.

Lance laughed. "Looks like he's eyeing you now, Trev. Dude must be gay or something."

Trevor and Robbie laughed at Lance's quip.

"So which is it," Trevor asked. "You eyeing my girl or you eyeing me?"

Mike knew better than to answer, even if it were to say neither. He had seen how these things go.

"Answer me, nerd," Trevor said, leaning forward, his face only inches from Mike's. There was a mean, hard look in his eyes.

Mike shrugged.

Trevor poked his chest with two fingers, causing Mike to flinch.

"Was that a shrug? You saying you don't know who you were eyeing?"

Mike fought to remain still, but his shoulders betrayed him and shrugged again.

"Looks like he's confused," Lance said. "I think maybe he needs some help clearing his head."

An unpleasant smile formed on Trevor's lips. "Well now. I think I know just the thing to help."

Before Mike could react, Trevor grabbed his shoulders

and spun him around, wrenching his right arm behind his back. In the mirror, Mike could see the twisted pleasure on Trevor's face for a split second before he was dragged to the first stall. Trevor shoved him face-first into the stall door, knocking it open, then kicked the back of Mike's knees, causing his legs to buckle and sending him to the floor, kneeling in front of the toilet. Trevor still had Mike's arm pinned behind his back. With his free hand, he grabbed Mike's hair and began pushing him forward. Mike tensed and tried to push back, but it was no use. He took a quick breath and closed his eyes as Trevor drove his head into the water in the bowl. Mike wasn't sure how long he was held under, but it felt like an eternity. When Trevor yanked his head up, Mike coughed and sputtered.

"How about that?" Trevor said, laughing. "That help clear your head? Now do you remember who you were staring at?"

Mike didn't say a thing. He knew if he opened his mouth, Trevor would immediately shove his face back in the water.

"I think he likes it," one of the others said. Mike wasn't sure which one, but it didn't matter. Trevor dunked him in again.

When he yanked him back up, Mike choked once more.

Trevor leaned down, his mouth next to Mike's ear. "Listen up, nerd. I ever catch you eyeing my girl again, I ain't gonna be so nice about it. Got it, nerd?"

Mike nodded.

Trevor gave him a shove as he released his arm. "Let's go," he said. The three of them left, laughing.

Mike heard the stall door at the far end open.

"Is it safe?" Graham whispered.

Still on his knees, Mike pulled a good amount of toilet paper from the dispenser and attempted to dry himself. His tie and the front of his shirt were soaked, as was his hair.

"You okay?" Graham asked from behind him.

Mike stood and brushed past him. He went to the sink and splashed water on his face, then grabbed a handful of paper towels and dried off as Graham stood by, watching.

When he had done what he could, he still looked wet.

"I'm going home," he said. He left the bathroom and headed for the exit, hoping no one would see him. When he entered the lobby, Trevor and his cronies were there, talking and laughing. Kayla and two other cheerleaders were with them.

"Check this guy out," Lance snickered.

Mike tried to keep his head down as he walked by them, but he couldn't. He looked up at Trevor, who wore a smirk on his face. Next to him, Kayla had a much different look on hers. Maybe it was concern, maybe it was pity. Either way, Mike never should have looked.

"Uh oh, he's eyeing your girl again, Trev," said Robbie.

Everyone laughed except Kayla.

"Hey, dick," Trevor said, stepping toward him. "I told

you to quit staring at my girl." He gave Mike a shove that sent him to the ground, landing hard on his backside. As he hit, he heard someone yell for Trevor to stop, but Trevor strode forward and stood over him.

"Am I going to have to dunk you in the toilet again, nerd? What are you, stupid? You didn't learn your lesson the first time?"

Kayla appeared at Trevor's side and yanked on his arm.

"Leave him alone," she said as she slid in between the two of them, her back to Mike. He could still see Trevor looking around her, his eyes drilling into him.

"You better watch yourself, nerd," Trevor said.

"Leave him alone," Kayla repeated, putting both her hands on his chest to hold him back. She was no match for him, but he stayed put. He glared at Mike a moment longer, then said, "Fine."

As Mike got up, aware that a small crowd was forming around them, Kayla turned and reached for his arm to help him. He shrugged her off, spun around and walked away as quickly as he could without running. Behind him, he heard more laughter.

Mike gasped and opened his eyes, raised his head and blinked several times. He wasn't sure what woke him, didn't think he had been having a dream but couldn't be certain. Whatever it was, something wasn't right. It took a moment to figure out what it was. The nightlight was off. The room wasn't pitch black, but it wasn't far from it. He groaned, dropped his head back onto the pillow, and decided he would worry about it in the morning.

He closed his eyes and began replaying the evening in his mind, but a noise chased all thoughts away. He tensed, kept his eyes shut and listened, telling himself that his ears had played a trick on him, that he hadn't heard what he thought he heard, out in the hall, which was the soft scuff of a footstep followed by the creaking of the floor.

The moments stretched out as he listened. Hearing nothing more, he relaxed. Maybe, just to put his mind at ease, he would turn on the light. Tomorrow, he could pick up another nightlight, maybe one that wasn't so cheap. Or maybe he could quit being a big baby, quit imagining things, and just go to sleep.

And then the floor creaked again. Every hair on his body stood up and tingled. For the first time he could recall, the creaking had come from right there in the room.

He held his breath, not moving a muscle as he opened his eyes and scanned the darkness. It was too black to see anything.

He told himself to quit being ridiculous, to just get up and turn on the light, but before he could move, the floor creaked again. And this time, he swore it was closer than the last.

It creaked again, definitely closer. He squinted into the darkness in the direction the sound had come from.

The floor creaked again, closer still and louder, and

he saw something move. He screamed and jumped to his feet, the covers tangling around him as he stumbled to the light switch, swinging his fists to fend off whatever was there. He crashed into the wall, searched frantically for the switch before finding it and turning on the light. He spun around, fists raised, expecting to see someone, or something, in the room with him, but nothing was there.

He began breathing again as he leaned against the wall, telling himself he was an idiot. Of course nothing was there. He had simply let his imagination get carried away.

He picked up the covers from the floor and tossed them back onto the bed, then crawled in, leaving the light on.

The next morning, Mike managed to get some work done despite a lack of sleep. After his near heart attack in the middle of the night, he had only dozed for a short while, and that wasn't until dawn. Still, he found energy in a cup of coffee and the fact that he had something to look forward to.

As he worked, he took a short break to gather the sheets from the bed. After dragging them across the floor in the middle of the night, and unable to recall the last time he had run them through the wash, he figured it was time.

A few minutes before eleven, he shut down his laptop and grabbed the clean sheets to put back on the bed. After tucking the corners and smoothing out the wrinkles, he left and drove to the library.

Audrey was in her office, phone pressed to her ear. When she saw him, she waved and held up a finger.

Mike grabbed a magazine from the periodicals shelf and sat at an empty table. He was three paragraphs into an article about a man wrongly imprisoned for 23 years when Audrey came out.

"You look like crap." She wore the same grin she always wore, had the usual impish look on her face.

"Is this how you treat all your patrons?"

"Just you." She sat down across from him.

Mike closed the magazine and tossed it onto the table. "Do you remember Kayla Warner?"

Audrey's grin faltered as she slowly nodded. "Of course I remember."

"I ran into her at the grocery store the other day."

"I heard her mother passed away a few weeks back."

"Yeah, she did."

"And Kayla's still in town?"

Mike nodded. "She had to come back to deal with the estate. Clean out the house."

Audrey studied him closer, her eyes squinting. "How do you know this?"

"I told you, I ran into her in the grocery store." He looked down as he said it.

"You talked to her?"

He nodded.

"Did she..."

He looked up. "Did she... what?"

Audrey shifted in her chair, appeared uncomfortable, which was a rarity. "Did she, you know, saying anything about..." She was trying to be as delicate as possible, yet still get the scoop.

"No."

"What did you talk about?"

Mike couldn't help but grin.

"What?" Audrey said, a trace of her usual self returning.

"Why so nosy?"

Audrey fake gasped and put a hand to her chest. "I am not nosy."

"You most definitely are. Anyway, I asked what brought her to town and she told me." He paused for dramatic effect. "Then she invited me to dinner."

Audrey gasped for real. "What? Please tell me you're kidding."

"I'm not."

"When was this?"

"Two nights ago."

Audrey stood, walked around the table and slapped him on the arm. "You're just now telling me? And why on earth would you go to dinner with her?"

"Because she's hot," Mike said, through a grin.

Audrey rolled her eyes. "Oh my god." She turned and walked away. Mike jumped up and followed her to her office.

"Close the door," she told him.

As soon as it was shut, she threw her arms in the air. "Why would you go to dinner with her?"

Mike held up both hands. "Easy there. We just talked for a minute in the store, she asked if I knew any place open to eat, I said yes, she asked if I wanted to go along. She just didn't want to sit in a restaurant alone is all."

Audrey's eyes narrowed as she glared at him. "I know what you're thinking, and you need to knock it off."

Mike laughed. "What am I thinking?"

"Probably the same thing you were thinking in high school. It got you into trouble then, and it'll do the same now."

She glared at him a moment longer before her expression softened.

"Look," she said, "I know the last year had been tough. But just..." She searched for the appropriate words but Mike stopped her before she found them.

"I get it. Don't worry."

They started with the pizza, then set about emptying closets, packing boxes, and stacking them along the wall. They saved the master bedroom for last, working their way through clothes, shoes, and a myriad of accessories. The conversation stayed light and meaningless, an easy back and forth that surprised Mike to no end. If it were 25 years ago, he would have been unable to speak or move.

They stopped for a short breather and sat on a wooden trunk at the end of the bed.

"What are you going to do with all of this?" Mike asked.

Kayla sighed. "Good question. The clothes I'll donate to Goodwill. I'll keep the stuff that reminds me of Mom, find a place for it. Everything else... I don't know."

A heaviness settled over them and Mike felt like an outsider. Surely there was someone else that should be here with her. Where was her husband? Other family? He wanted to ask but knew the timing was awful. He felt for her, losing her mom and having to sort through her life with an almost perfect stranger. It wasn't right.

"I'm really sorry," he said. "You shouldn't have to be doing this alone."

She was silent, unmoving for a long moment, before turning and grinning. "In case you haven't noticed, I'm not the only one here."

He matched her grin. "True. But what I meant was —"

"I know," she interrupted. "I know."

The silence stretched out, but it wasn't awkward. The situation seemed to require a moment of quiet, time to gather thoughts and figure out how to keep moving.

Kayla tapped the chest they were on. "Let's see what's in here, shall we?"

They stood and she lifted the lid. Inside were piles of scrapbooks, stacks of photos, a graduation gown and cap, cheerleader uniform, tiara, various pieces of the history only a mom would keep of her daughter.

"Oh my..." Kayla clamped a hand over her mouth, then lifted a scrapbook from the top and opened it.

Sixth Grade.

As she flipped through the pages, her 12-year-old self stared back, laughing and smiling, playing and having fun. There were pictures of her with friends, with the family dog, and pictures with her mom. Hand-drawn hearts were sprinkled about on each page.

"I haven't seen these things in so long."

Her cheeks were wet with tears as she neared the end. She stopped on a page with pictures of her and her classmates wearing large paper collars pinned around their necks, covering their shoulders and adorned with a red crêpe ribbon fixed to the front. The entire ensemble looked like a Puritan shawl with a red bow tie.

"The Christmas program," she said. "I almost forgot about that." A fresh tear spilled down her cheek.

For Mike, the photo brought back a rush of memories. The Christmas program was a yearly tradition where all students, kindergarten through sixth, were lined up in the bleachers of the gym to sing Christmas songs to the parents seated below in row upon row of folding chairs. It was the highlight of every year, a day when the students didn't have to study lessons, didn't have to conform to the normal rules of the classroom. They only had to remember the words to songs they had heard their entire lives. Best of all, it was the last day before winter break and was the official signal that Christmas was finally within reach. It was magical. Each year Mike would search the faces below for his parents, would always find them along with his grandpa.

And then one year they weren't there. He had searched every face as he mouthed the words to the songs, too shy to sing out loud. Each pass he made, he expected to see them. Surely he was just missing them. Maybe they were toward the back. When the program was over, he still hadn't found them.

Back in the classroom, he and his classmates moved about unfettered and free from the bonds of their desks. Chatter and laughter filled the air as collars were un-pinned and everyone prepared to head home for the break, to experience the joys of Christmas. Mike was laughing with his friends when he had finally seen his mom walk into the classroom and speak with the teacher. The teacher had placed a hand on his mom's arm. When they both turned, looked across the room at him, he knew something was wrong.

"Are you okay?" Kayla asked.

Mike snapped back to the present, realizing his cheeks now matched hers. He wiped at his eyes and sniffled. "Yeah, sorry."

"What is it?" she asked, her eyes filled with both tears and concern. Just like his mom's and his teacher's had been.

"Nothing." He wiped at his cheeks again. "Sorry."

"Stop apologizing," she said, her tone gentle. "What is it?"

She still held the scrapbook open. One of the photos was a wide shot of the assembly, capturing most of the students in the stands, lined up in their matching collars.

The tops of parents' heads filled the bottom foreground. Mike was somewhere in that sea of kids.

He sniffed again and found his voice, pointed to the photo. Captured there were the last moments of his life that had yet to experience loss on a large scale.

"I was in fourth grade here. This was the day my grandfather passed away."

Kayla's smile was kind and sad. "I'm so sorry," she whispered, closing the scrapbook and placing it back in the trunk.

Mike searched for something to say to lighten the moment. He picked up the cheerleader uniform, unfolded it and held it up. "Well, I definitely remember this."

Kayla laughed first, a short snort, then another, then they were both laughing.

They worked until dark, leaving only the barest of essentials untouched. Things like a single set of dishes in the kitchen, sheets and pillows on the bed in Kayla's old room, where she had been sleeping. The rest was labeled and packed away, ready for wherever it would go next.

"I admire your organizational skills," Mike said as they rested on opposite ends of the couch.

"Thanks."

Not far in, they had settled into a groove, Kayla labeling and directing, handling the delicate items, Mike doing the rest along with the heavy lifting. When it came to the chest, they had left it as it was. Kayla decided she would load it into the car and take it with her when she returned to Indianapolis, it's cargo too precious to trust with anyone else. The rest would be shipped, donated, or thrown away.

After a daylong cacophony of packing and talking, the room was silent and still. Mike's stomach growled, practically echoing through the house. He clamped his hands over his midsection as they both laughed.

"Come on," Kayla said, standing up. "I'm buying dinner."

"You don't have to do —"

She held up a hand and cut him off. "I insist. I owe you. Plus, it would do me good to get out of here for a while."

They were the last to leave Cane's, minutes before closing time. Outside on the sidewalk, the warm air surrounded them. Several cars rolled by, their headlights on and their interiors dark. As they strolled toward Mike's Jeep, Kayla glanced at her watch.

"Sorry I've kept you out so late."

Mike waved a dismissive hand. "No worries. My curfew isn't until 11."

"Good. I'd hate to get you in trouble," she said, grinning.

When they reached the Jeep, Kayla stopped by the front fender and turned, looking back to the intersection of Main and Broadway a block down. She sighed, small and almost unnoticeable, but Mike caught it. Following her gaze, he watched the stoplight turn from red to green. A waiting car moved on, disappearing around the corner.

The street was well lit and when she turned back toward him, Mike could easily see the lights reflecting in her eyes and had to remind himself not to stare.

He pulled his keys out, unlocked the passenger door. As he opened it, he stopped halfway.

"Everything okay?" he asked.

Her smile was subtle as she nodded. "Of course. I'm just not dying to get back to Mom's house."

Mike waited as she averted her eyes and fidgeted with her hands.

"I don't know," she finally continued, "there's just something about being there alone at night. It's too quiet." She paused to search for more words. "I miss her. I feel it more at night, I guess."

Mike understood all too well. The things that got lost in the noise and commotion of the day came to the forefront once night fell and the world grew quiet. Although, in his case, the night never grew *entirely* quiet. There was always the creaking.

He reached in, locked the door, and pushed it back closed.

"You know what? There's no need to head back right away. How about we go for a walk around the block, waste some time?"

Kayla's smile widened a touch. "Sure. Sounds good."

They headed south, away from Main, the ambient light from the street fading behind them. The sky overhead was clear, no clouds stood between them and the moon. A breeze stirred, dislodging a strand of hair from behind Kayla's ear. She tucked it back in and looked up.

"It's so beautiful out tonight. I can't remember the last time I went for a walk after dark."

Mike stuffed his hands into his pockets and turned his focus to the cracks in the sidewalk passing beneath his feet. "Summer nights are the best."

Beside him, Kayla took a deep breath, like she was trying to inhale a piece of the night to carry with her. Mike wanted to look, to see how beautiful she was in the soft light of the moon, but he kept his eyes on the sidewalk.

"The world feels so different at night," she said. "I can't explain it."

"I agree." He threw caution to the wind and risked a brief look in her direction, confirming his suspicions. She was radiant. "When I was a kid, there was nothing better than being out in the neighborhood after dark. It was like another world. The look, the feel, the smell. It changed at night."

Kayla stopped, so Mike stopped too, turning toward her.

"Exactly," she said as her face lit up. "It was like stumbling into this place that was familiar, yet different, like the world at large no longer existed, like it was just you and where you were." She shook her head and wrinkled her nose. "I'm not explaining this very well."

"You are," Mike said, trying not to stare. He understood perfectly.

She looked at the darkened windows of the hardware store across the street and frowned. "I can't remember when I stopped noticing."

Sadness covered her face like a shadow. It was there only a moment, then fled, replaced by a half smile.

"I guess it's a casualty of growing up," she added.

"I guess so."

They resumed their walk, Mike returning his attention to the concrete.

When they reached the end of the block, they turned left, ambling slowly toward Broadway. They passed the buildings that once housed the tiny fire station and the local newspaper but was now a shop that sold cupcakes.

At Broadway, they paused. On the other side, the Coleman Theater stood dark and silent, its doors closed for the last time years ago.

Mike nodded in its direction. "Did you ever go see movies there?" He already knew the answer.

"Of course. You?"

"Almost every weekend, I think."

He remembered seeing her there a handful of times. She had disappeared altogether when he was 14 as she and her friends had started driving, choosing their new-found freedom over the old theater. It would be the same for him two years later.

"Do you remember a guy named Joe that was always

there with the Human Development Center folks?" she asked.

"Are you kidding?" Mike said, grinning as the memories flooded in. "Of course I remember Joe. He was a permanent fixture, practically an institution. Anyone who knew the Coleman knew Joe."

A single car drove past as they studied the empty marquee jutting out over the sidewalk.

"It's funny," Kayla said, "I haven't thought about the Coleman in years. Maybe decades. But I remember Joe, maybe more than anything else."

They stood shoulder to shoulder and offered up a moment of silence. The old theater, first built in the 1930s, had been the center of countless memories for so many, just like the thousands of other small-town theaters across the nation had been for their own communities. And then, one day, the world had moved on without them.

"I wonder what happened to him," Kayla said, finally breaking the silence. "Do you think he's still around?"

Mike didn't answer right away; he was being tugged back through time. He was sitting in the theater, watching groups of kids from school laughing and talking together, waiting for the movie, a sci-fi action flick, to start. From the moment he had seen the trailer weeks before, he knew he had to watch it. *Had* to. But none of his friends could make it. And so he sat there, the only person in the theater with no one next to him, trying to sink far enough into the seat to become invisible. Awkward and alone, he wished the houselights would just go out already, hoped none of the kids from school noticed him there, by himself.

But someone had noticed. It was Joe. He had sat down next to Mike and smiled, kept him company, and before Mike knew it, the lights went out and the movie started.

It was always like that with Joe. Every regular had likely been singled out by him at one point or another, had gained an unexpected member of their party for the duration of a movie. The way Mike remembered it, everyone liked Joe, even with his extra chromosome. Probably because of it. He wore his childlike joy and wonder on his sleeve, for all to see, never met a movie he didn't like.

Mike snapped back to the present and could feel Kayla's eyes on him, waiting for him to speak.

"Wherever he is," he finally answered, "I hope he's happy."

He glanced at her long enough to see the streetlights in her eyes again, then looked down at his feet.

"I hope so, too," she said.

They resumed walking, heading back toward Main. From the corner of his eye, he watched her study the old buildings, some housing new businesses, some empty.

"You know," she said, "I've been so focused on Mom's house that I haven't paid close attention to the town and how much it's changed. And how much it hasn't."

Mike understood. Life could easily get in the way,

make you miss what was right in front of you. Remembering to stop and take a look at things now and again, to see past the debts and doubts and worries, was a hard thing to do.

They came to the stoplight, the intersection empty. Turning left, they headed back to where they started.

When they reached the Jeep, Mike opened the passenger door, waited for her to climb in and get situated.

"Fingers and toes," he said, then closed the door. She was grinning at him when he hopped into the driver seat.

"What?" he asked.

"Fingers and toes?"

He laughed. "Oh yeah. Right. It's something my mom used to say when I was a kid. Apparently, one time, my finger got shut in the car door. After that, she always warned me to keep my fingers and toes clear. It became a normal thing, like saying 'God bless you' after a sneeze."

Her smiled widened as she buckled her seat belt. "That's sweet."

Minutes later, as they pulled into the driveway, Kayla yawned and leaned back against the headrest.

"The day's catching up with me," she said. "Maybe I'll get lucky and be asleep the moment I hit the pillow."

Mike was tired as well, could feel it in his bones, but it was a good kind of tired, the kind that came with a hard day's work and a feeling of accomplishment. It had been a while.

Kayla yawned a second time. "Thanks again for all your help. I'm lucky I ran into you in the grocery store."

Mike smiled and nodded. He wanted to say *me too* but kept it to himself.

"Maybe we can grab a bite to eat again before I leave," she said.

"Sounds good," Mike answered, though it sounded better than good. Much better.

She opened the door and climbed out. "Good night."

"Good night."

Mike watched as she walked to the porch, unlocked the door, and disappeared inside. After the light in the living room window came on and the porch light went off, he shifted into reverse.

Back in his own driveway, he sat in the Jeep, staring at the darkened bedroom window. He was tired and his head was foggy from the long day, but he was certain he had left the bedroom light on, had made of point of it when he left. There was no way he had wanted to come home to a dark bedroom. Especially after last night.

"I hate this house," he mumbled to himself as he got out and walked to the porch. He paused to take a deep breath, not ready to go in and listen to the symphony of creaking that awaited him.

When he finally opened the door and slipped inside, he considered the upstairs landing, the darkness of the hallway at the end, and decided he would sleep on the couch.

26 Years Earlier

Mike watched as the headlights approached and swung into the drive, raking across him before coming to a rest on the house and blinking off. The car engine ran for a second more, then stopped.

He considered going inside, the last thing he wanted was to talk to anyone, but he stayed put.

Audrey climbed out of the car, closing the door gently behind her. She didn't speak as she stepped up onto the porch and sat down on the front edge of the empty chair beside him.

Mike kept his gaze turned toward the darkened yard, not wanting her to see the embarrassment, anger, and hurt that swirled over his face.

Before long, Audrey slid back in the chair, situating her dress.

"Are you okay?" she asked, her voice barely above a whisper.

Mike wasn't sure how to answer, but his silence must have told her all she needed to know.

"Those guys are assholes," she said. "One of these days they'll get what's coming to them."

Mike wanted to laugh, but was afraid of what it might turn into.

"Did I ever tell you that Lance hit on me one time?"

It didn't surprise Mike. Audrey was beautiful, funny, and smart. Too smart to fall for the advances of someone like Lance.

"I shot him down, of course," she continued. "Then he just started acting like I was the one hitting on him and that he wasn't interested. Got all defensive. What an idiot."

A small grin found its way onto Mike's lips.

"I feel I should warn you about something, though," Audrey said.

"What's that?" Mike asked, feeling confident enough to speak.

"Before I left the dance, I let the air out of one of Trevor's tires."

Mike turned and searched her face for any signs she was joking. Surely she was, but it wasn't showing in her expression.

"You did not," he said.

"I did." She held up her hands to show the smudges of dirt still there.

A short laugh escaped as Mike eyed her. "Holy crap. You really did, didn't you?"

She nodded as a smile spread across her face, then melted away. "I didn't really think it through, I just did it. Now, I'm worried he might think it was you."

Mike smiled and leaned back in his chair, looking out at the night. "You are a serious badass."

Audrey giggled, a sound that was uniquely hers. "I kind of am."

They stayed quiet for a long moment before Mike spoke.

"You didn't have to leave the dance."

"Yeah, I did."

Mike let the silence stretch out again before continuing.

"You wanna go back and let the air out the rest of them?"

Audrey's giggle returned. "We probably shouldn't push our luck."

"You're right," Mike said. "We probably shouldn't."

A full minute passed before Audrey said, "But let's do it anyway."

When Mike woke up, his back was stiff and his muscles ached. The living room and kitchen lights were still on, but a quick glance at the window told him the world outside remained dark. He checked his phone for the time. 3:27am.

The decision to avoid the darkened upstairs when he had returned home from helping Kayla had seemed like a good idea at the time, but now, hours later, he wasn't so sure. The couch wasn't the most comfortable piece of furniture in the world.

Somewhere upstairs, the house creaked. Mike yawned and decided he had chosen well after all. He closed his eyes and pretended he wasn't hearing a thing. It was almost working until he heard the thump. Creaks and groans were a dime a dozen, but thumps were not. He held his breath and listened.

It sounded again as he sat up and looked into the kitchen. Did it come from that direction? He wasn't sure. Taking a deep breath to calm the beating of his heart, he listened until he heard it again. There was a faraway quality to it, yet close at the same time.

Another thump.

Maybe it was the central heat and air unit.

Another one. They were coming in a rhythm now.

Mike stood and walked toward the kitchen in slow, light steps.

Thump.

He stopped in the large arched opening between the two rooms.

Thump.

The noise was definitely coming from the kitchen area. He took a few steps in, waited.

Thump.

Mike realized it wasn't coming from *inside* the kitchen, but *below*. He listened intently, heard the thump again. When he took another step, the floor creaked beneath his foot. He froze, the house suddenly as quiet as he had ever heard it. He waited for the next thump, the next beat of the rhythm, but it never came. Ten excruciating minutes later, he gave up and returned to the couch. Whatever it had been, it stopped. Maybe he should in-vestigate further, but there was no way in hell he was going down to the basement. And besides, the only entrance was outside, behind the house, a fact for which he was now extremely grateful. If there had been a door to the basement inside the house, he would have abandoned ship altogether, gone to Audrey's and told her his rent house had burned to the ground or some other such story, whatever it took to convince her to let him sleep on her couch. As it was, he stayed put, telling himself he was a grown-up.

At 8am, Mike gave up on sleep. He fixed breakfast, keeping his mind off the basement below as he sat at the kitchen table with his laptop, working as he ate.

Around 10am, the empty plate still on the table, he added the finishing touches to the project, and with that, he was out of work. No other projects had come in, and he certainly hadn't gone looking for any. Usually, he would have other jobs lined up, waiting in the queue, but motivation had been hard to come by the past year and, as a result, the work had run out.

After putting away the dishes, he went upstairs, slowing as he approached the bedroom. The door was open, the room coming into view as he inched toward it. The hairs on the back of his neck stood and he braced himself, for what he wasn't sure. All he knew was that the creepy feelings he got at night were now spilling over into the day. That was not a good sign. Not a good sign at all.

He stopped and took a shaky breath and held it,

telling himself he was being ridiculous, something he was doing a lot of lately. So far, it hadn't worked.

He crept forward, expecting to see a figure come into view, just a sliver at first, then more, but the room was empty. He stood in the door and resumed breathing, checked the light switch and found it in the off position. As he was about to turn away, the bed caught his eye. He stared at it for a moment before going back downstairs, where he sat on the couch and racked his brain, trying to remember if he had made the bed the previous day. He felt like he had, but he couldn't remember for sure. For the most part, he only made the bed after washing the sheets, so it stood to reason he had stuck to the routine yesterday. But now, he was doubting himself.

Whatever the case, the bed was currently an unmade mess.

"I think the place is haunted."

"Haunted, huh?" Audrey asked, a dubious look on her face. There was also the hint of a smile; she obviously thought he was joking. "What makes you say that?"

Mike shrugged. He'd had it in mind to tell her everything, in great detail, but he held back. He could imagine how it would sound. The last thing he wanted was for Audrey to think he was losing his mind. She would inevitably tie it back to the divorce, would think he was having a nervous breakdown. She might even rope him into to seeing a psychiatrist.

"I don't know," he said. "It's the usual, I guess. Strange noises, things like that. And it just feels creepy sometimes."

"Have you been, you know —" She tilted her head back and raised an imaginary bottle to her mouth. Mike waited as she gulped loudly three times.

"I'm serious," he said. "Something is going on there."

"Sure."

Mike sighed. "All right then, you spend the night there by yourself. Just one night. And then tell me there's no such thing as haunted houses."

"I'm not going to spend the night there," she scoffed. "That would be weird."

"Weird, or frightening?"

"Weird. Besides, it's an old house. They make noises."

Mike crossed his arms and tilted his head to the side as he studied her. "You're afraid, aren't you?"

"No, I'm not afraid."

Her answer was too quick and too loud.

"Yep, you're definitely scared."

"I am not," Audrey said, her face a mask of pretend disbelief.

"Then pack a bag and stay over this weekend. I'll stay at your place."

She scoffed once more. "That's ridiculous. We aren't trading houses. By the way, we have cookies today."

"What kind?"

"Your favorite."

Mike grabbed her shoulders and steadied her, looking

her directly in the eye. "You better not be toying with me, woman."

She smiled and nodded. "Double chocolate."

"Sweet baby Jesus." He let her go, spun around, and headed for the breakroom, her laughter trailing behind him.

"I'm limiting you to two," she called out.

"I can't hear you," he replied, deciding to drop his concerns about the house for now.

Back at the house, Mike sat on the couch, staring at the wall. Oddly enough, after talking to Audrey, he felt better. It was as though the idea of the house actually being haunted was rendered ridiculous just by saying it out loud.

Of course it was ridiculous. And as for the bed, maybe he hadn't made it like he thought. Maybe he had started, stretched the fitted sheet into place, then got side-tracked. He had, after all, been looking forward to seeing Kayla, so he was certainly distracted. He could have easily left it unmade while his thoughts had wandered.

It was a reasonable explanation. There was likely one to be had in the basement as well. Perhaps it would do him good to take a look, see what it held firsthand rather than letting his imagination run wild. He made up his mind, stood and headed out the front door.

The sun hung overhead in a cloudless sky, but the narrow side yard was shaded by two large trees. A row of scraggly bushes gave the illusion of a barrier between the house and the road that ran beside it. Mold covered parts of the wooden siding, and the ground held only sparse grass and dead leaves. The smell of decay and soil was strong, seemed to hang in place. Toward the back corner was a low spot in the ground, damp and soft. It probably spent most of the year filled with standing water.

The backyard was almost nonexistent, just a short space between the house and an alleyway running between it and the back of the courthouse. The bushes lining this end of the yard were thick and unkept, but there were gaps through which the courthouse could be seen.

Halfway along the back of the house, a small set of concrete steps led up to the backdoor, which opened into the kitchen. Just past that, the angled cellar entrance jutted out from the house, covered by two tin doors. There was no latch that Mike could see, nothing but gravity holding them shut. He grabbed the edge of one and pulled, lifting it. The hinges squeaked and wailed.

Wooden steps led down into the dark. Mike squinted, but was unable to see much past the bottom step. All he knew for sure was that the floor was dirt and the smell of decaying earth was strong. Beyond that was a mystery. If he was going to go in, he would need a flashlight, which he didn't have. He lowered the door back into place and returned to the front yard. Exploring the depths of the basement would have to wait.

Mike recognized the song playing overhead, tried his best to tune it out. That was the problem with music. It pulled you into memories without regard to whether they were good or bad. This one was bad.

Paying no attention to the brand, he grabbed a tube of sausage and package of bacon. Might as well cover all the breakfast meats.

In normal times, he would get milk, but he wanted a reason to come back tomorrow, to get out of the house; there was still enough for one more bowl of cereal.

He took his meager haul to the front, where Monotone Checkout Girl was leaning against the register, studying her fingernails. She turned when Mike sat his basket on the conveyer.

"Hey, Mr. Ellerton. Did you find everything all right?" She peered into his basket, then stared at him with her usual blank face.

"Yep."

She rang up the two items, told him his total.

"How did the algebra test go?" he asked as he handed over a twenty.

"Fine." She gave him his change and bagged the two items.

"Just fine? What did you make?"

She offered her usual stare before answering. It had taken him a while to get used to that, but he now knew to wait it out, just stare back.

"97."

Mike did his best not to react, except to give a

slight nod. One thing he had learned was that Monotone Checkout Girl did not take compliments well. He had to keep it low-key, not make a big deal.

"Good job," he said, as subdued as he could make it.

"Whatever."

He grabbed his bag. "Have a good evening."

As he walked away, he heard her say, "You, too... Mr. Ellerton."

Kids these days.

That night, as Mike stared at the muted TV screen, he thought about Kayla and wondered how she was doing with the rest of the packing. When he had left the night before, he hadn't offered to come back for a third straight day, hadn't wanted to wear out his welcome. A part of him hoped she would ask, but that didn't happen.

Maybe it was for the best. What good was it doing anyway? She was married. There was no way in hell she was interested in him, not in any romantic sense. Even if she was, he knew firsthand how it felt to be on the crappy end of that deal. He couldn't do that to someone else.

Granted, they had shared a few nice moments. The trunk full of childhood memories, the walk around the block. But they were just that, nice moments. Nothing else. Anything more would be a cruel joke played on him by the universe. A cruel joke indeed. To continue would only serve to torment him.

His phone dinged, signaling the arrival of a text message. It was from Audrey.

Seen any ghosts tonight?

The girl was a regular comedian.

Just the ghost of our dead friendship, he replied.

Very funny.

There was a pause before the next message came in.

If you need anything, you know how to reach me.

He smiled. That was Audrey, always looking out for him, had been for as long as he could remember. She had called him every day during his divorce, had picked him up when he was at his lowest, helped him keep his chin up when all he had wanted was to hang his head and let the waves of despair carry him out to sea.

He typed a message and hit send.

Who is this? How did you get this number?

Occasionally, he overcompensated, joked around too much while trying to show her he was all right, even when he wasn't. *Especially* when he wasn't.

She sent back an eye roll emoji, followed by another message.

I'm bringing donuts to work in the morning. I'll save you a few.

He replied, *You are a godsend.*

I know. Sleep tight, don't let the ghosts bite.

Mike sighed and typed out his response.

I regret telling you things.

And yet you always do it.

She had him there.

Good night.

Good night.

He sat the phone aside and eyed the upstairs landing. The bedroom light was on, just as he had left it before running to the store. Still, he wasn't keen on going up. He unmuted the TV, watched for a while, then picked up the phone and typed out a message. He hovered over the delete key, telling himself he should quit while he was ahead. Instead of listening to reason, he tapped the send icon.

How did it go today? Did you make good progress?

A full, agonizing minute passed before a reply came back.

It went well, didn't overdo it, but made progress. Good news! One of the neighbors is buying the living room set. He's coming by at noon tomorrow. Hopefully we can wrestle everything out of here. LOL

Mike hesitated, realized he might be a glutton for punishment.

That's great! If you want, I can stop by and help move it.

Are you sure? I hate to keep taking up your time.

Unknown to her, time was something he had in abundance.

It's no problem. I've got the day off.

Perfect! Thank you so much! I owe you!!

The delusional 16-year-old kid in Mike that thought he had a chance with the homecoming queen was ecstatic. The adult in him, however, knew he should stop the torment and get back to reality, as much as that reality sucked right now.

Sounds great, he responded, then tossed his phone onto the table and sighed.

There would be time later to stop torturing himself.

The old man scratched at his thin gray hair. His expression suggested he had wandered into the wrong house only to realize he wasn't home.

"I imagine me and you could lift it out of here, don't ya think?"

Mike nodded, though he was thinking the exact opposite. The man was frail, likely pushing 80, both in age and weight. He was nice, with kind eyes and a pleasant voice, but he wasn't made for lifting couches, at least not anymore.

"You know," Kayla said, "I think me and Mike can get it. How about you direct us, Mr. Massey?"

Before Mr. Massey could speak, Mike said, "Good idea, I'll grab this end."

Mr. Massey objected, claiming he was still spry enough to move furniture, but Kayla insisted, offering up her best smile. He melted at the sight of it and relented.

Mr. Massey held the door as Mike backed his way onto the porch, taking it slow and easy down the steps. Kayla held her own, didn't seem too fazed by the weight.

Mr. Massey's truck sat in the drive, looking as though it had arrived straight from 1954. He had bought it used 52 years ago, his first major purchase as a young man. $200, he had said when Mike asked about it. It had seen him through five decades of marriage, three kids, seven grandkids, and 16 great grandkids.

Mike lifted his end of the couch into the bed, then helped Kayla slide it forward until it touched the cab.

Mr. Massey climbed in, fired up the engine, and drove to his house two doors down, arriving several minutes after Kayla and Mike, who had walked at a slow pace. They unloaded the couch and left it under the carport. Mr. Massey's grandsons would come by later to help him move it inside and get the old couch out.

They made a second trip, moving the two chairs and the coffee table. When finished, Mr. Massey thanked them, squeezed Kayla's hand and said he was sorry, that her mother had been a fine woman and a wonderful neighbor.

As they walked back to the house, Kayla was quiet. When they entered the empty living room, she wiped at her eyes.

"You know what sounds good?" Mike said. "Ice cream."

Kayla glanced at him, then back to the empty room. "I could use a break."

Mike nudged her with his elbow and tilted his head toward the door. "Let's go."

They took his Jeep to Jackson's Café on Broadway, a block up from the Coleman. They ate lunch first, then each ordered a large bowl of ice cream.

As they ate, Kayla seemed to shed the weight of the empty living room, returning to something closer to her old self, or at least what Mike knew that to be.

She dug into her bowl, flipped the spoon upside down and eyed the ice cream melded to it.

"There was somebody wearing a superhero costume standing on the corner yesterday," she said.

Mike nodded once as he concentrated on digging out his own spoonful.

"He's one of the new additions to the town since you've been gone." He put a hand on the bowl to hold it in place as he dug. "He was actually around back in high school, just not as a superhero. He would park here on Broadway on the weekends, watching all the cars go by. Always had a radio sitting next to him."

Kayla's eyes lit up in recognition. "I remember him. That's the same guy?"

Mike nodded. "He became the bat man years ago. I'm not sure why. I don't think I've seen him any other way since."

"Why does he do it?"

It was a good question, one that Mike didn't know

how to answer, so he shrugged. "Your guess is as good as mine."

Kayla stared out the window, watched a car pull into an empty, slanted parking spot. "It's peculiar, isn't it?"

Mike shrugged again. "Maybe. Maybe not. I mean, everyone hides behind a mask of some sort. Maybe his just happens to be a real one."

Their eyes met for a moment, and Mike could feel her stare piercing much deeper than he wanted. He dropped his gaze to the bowls between them.

"He's a good guy, though," Mike continued. "I heard there was this kid who was sick. The local fire stations, police, all of that, had a drive-by caravan. He went along for the ride, then came back the next day and brought the kid an action figure. No one asked him, he just did it."

Glancing up, he caught the hint of a smile on Kayla's face.

"That was sweet," she said.

"Yeah," Mike agreed. "It was."

Kayla placed her spoon in the bowl and crossed her arms on the table. "What do you think he's hiding behind his mask?"

Mike dropped his spoon as well and traced one of the squares of the checkered tablecloth with his index finger as he thought. "I don't know. Maybe the same as the rest of us."

"And what's that?"

Mike stayed focused on the square.

"The usual, probably," he answered. "Sadness. Heart-ache."

"How much is left?" Mike asked.

They were back at her mom's house, sitting at the kitchen table, groggy from lunch and ice cream.

Kayla slumped over, propped her head in her hand and sighed.

"More than I would like. I'll be cutting it close, but it's doable. I need to get the bathrooms finished up today because Goodwill is coming tomorrow to get all the boxes. They'll be back on Saturday for the remaining furniture. I'll hopefully have time on Monday and Tuesday to deal with the financial stuff, close accounts, cancel services, that kind of thing, and take care of any other loose ends that I've missed. Then I'll pack up the things I'm taking with me and hit the road Wednesday morning."

"Sound like a full schedule."

Kayla nodded. "Yes. But, I'd be hopelessly behind if it wasn't for you. I know I keep saying it, but I just can't thank you enough."

Mike dropped his eyes to the tabletop. "You're very welcome."

Silence hung in the air until Kayla sat up, sighed, and looked around the kitchen, then into the living room.

"Tomorrow and Saturday will be tough," she said. "It was hard seeing the living room furniture go, it'll be harder seeing the rest of it leave."

Mike studied her profile. Even with a partial view, he could see the sadness on her face. He knew firsthand it was difficult letting go, and though Kayla hadn't lived within these walls in decades, it was still her home. There was an entire childhood of memories floating inside, only now they were slowly leaking out.

The idea of her watching them go alone bothered Mike.

He slid his chair back and stood. "Come on, I'll give you a hand with the bathrooms."

Kayla turned toward him and smiled.

Hours later, they sat on the living room floor, the carpet well-worn and faded except where the furniture had been. Those squares and rectangles gave clues to the floor's original appearance, before the passage of time and countless feet had taken its toll on the rest. The bathrooms were done, the cleaning supplies boxed up. They had even gone out and looked in the shed, deciding to leave well enough alone there.

"I'm going to miss this place," Kayla said, mostly to herself.

Mike rubbed a hand across the shag next to his leg. "It's a nice place." He preferred not to push, but it seemed like a good opening. "You given any more thought to my offer?"

"Hmm?"

"To rent it, take care of the upkeep."

Kayla leaned back against the wall and stretched her legs out, staring across the room at nothing. Outside, daylight was fading fast.

"Honestly, I've had too much on my mind to think about it." Her head lolled over in his direction. "Sorry. But I'll definitely give it some thought."

"No worries," Mike said. "I understand." He pulled at the shag where the couch leg had been, trying to make it stand up. "But just so you know, the house I'm in now is haunted."

Kayla grinned and raised an eyebrow. "Is that so?"

"Yes. But don't let that sway your decision. Also, there's something in the basement. I'm not saying it's a monster, but —" he shrugged "— what else would it be?"

Kayla's grin widened. "Okay. I won't let that sway my decision."

They both quietly laughed until Mike took a deep breath, let it out, and climbed to his feet.

"I should get going."

Reaching down, he offered his hand. Kayla studied it a moment before taking it. Once upright, she brushed at the seat of her pants.

"Thanks again for your help."

He responded with a smile, and she followed him to the door and onto the porch. Small clouds hung overhead, barely lit by the last rays of the day.

"You need help with the Goodwill stuff tomorrow?" He stepped off the porch and turned back. Kayla leaned against the post and shoved her hands into the pockets of her jeans. In the dying light, she once again looked like a teenager.

"They said they would send three guys to do all the loading. I'll just be directing traffic."

"Sounds good," Mike said, though it didn't at all. "If anything comes up, if you need anything before you leave, you know how to reach me."

"I do," she said, her perfect smile returning. "And thank you once again for all your help. I couldn't have done it without you."

"Have a good night."

"You too. Watch out for monsters."

Mike laughed as he turned away, hoping it didn't sound forced.

Back at the house, Mike sat in the Jeep, engine still running, staring up at the darkened bedroom window. If he returned to Kayla's mom's, knocked on the door, explained to her that his jokes about the house hadn't really been jokes at all, would she think he was crazy? Would she laugh it off, assuming he was there for another reason?

With a sigh, he shut off the engine, but remained seated for several minutes before finding the nerve to open the door.

----

18 Months Earlier

Mike was having trouble holding the phone. His hand was shaking, and it was all he could do not to throw it across the room. Somehow, he held it, however unsteady, and was still holding it when Melissa walked in.

Her head was tilted sideways, her wet hair hanging over one shoulder as she ran a towel through it.

"Would you mind if we skipped —" She stopped when she saw Mike. "What are you doing?"

Mike didn't speak, didn't even look at her. His eyes were still on the phone. Its screen had gone black from inactivity, but he could still see the messages and the pictures as plain as day. He blinked several times, attempting to remove the images from his mind, but it did no good.

"Why do you have my phone?" she asked, forcing a smile.

Mike slowly placed the phone on the coffee table and stood.

"Who's Grant?"

"What? What do you mean?"

Mike faced her, studied her expression. She was playing dumb, every move overdone, pronounced, but Mike could see the truth written in her eyes, the same as he had seen it on her phone.

He walked past her.

"Wait," she said, following him down the hall to the bedroom.

He picked up his wallet and keys, then brushed past her again.

"Mike. Please. We need to talk."

"I'll come back for my things when you're not here," he said.

"Mike, wait. Let's talk." She caught up to him and grabbed his arm. Her touch was light, but it shot through him like a lightning strike.

He spun, causing her to take a step back. He was angry to the point of screaming, verbally lashing out with every bit of vitriol he could muster, but he held it in, smothered it with the hurt.

"I can explain," she said, her voice shaky. "I never meant to —"

He turned and walked away.

"Mike."

He ignored her as he left, pulling the door gently closed behind him.

Mike sighed as he stared at the TV and the time slipped past 1am. As much as he tried to avoid it, there were still those moments when the memories resurfaced, almost always at night. The images burned into his brain would return and he would force them away, only to sink deeper into the past.

The night he had walked out was the last time he had seen his home of 15 years. He hadn't returned for his things, but had sent Dave and Audrey instead. The days passed in a haze. Weeks turned to months until finally, one cold November morning, he found the energy to get dressed, drive to his lawyer's office, and sign the final papers. He had gone back to the apartment he was renting and cried until he had no more tears left. The next morning, he picked himself up and wondered what he was going to do with the rest of his life.

It wasn't supposed to be like this, sitting alone in a stranger's house. Nineteen years of marriage, of building a life, gone. His future plans gone as well. To top it off, he was chasing after the homecoming queen, who was, by the way, married.

He turned off the TV, tossed the remote aside, and climbed the stairs. With any luck, he would be murdered in his sleep.

CHAPTER

7

The moment Mike walked into the library, he knew he was in trouble.

"Where were you yesterday?" Audrey asked, a fake scowl creasing her forehead. "I saved you donuts."

"Something came up. You still have them?"

She jerked her head toward Chelsea, who sat behind the circulation desk checking in books.

Chelsea stopped mid-scan. "Was I not supposed to eat those?"

"Dammit, Chelsea," Mike said, trying to be stern but unable to keep from grinning. She laughed and returned to scanning.

"Serves you right," Audrey said. "Come with me."

Mike obeyed, followed her to her office where she closed the door and told him to sit down.

"Why do I feel like I'm in the principal's office?" Mike said.

Audrey sat behind her desk and gave him a look, her stare boring into him.

"What came up?"

"What do you mean?" Mike asked, stalling.

"You said something came up. What came up?"

Mike shrugged, scraped at the edge of her desk with his fingernail. "Just stuff."

"Oh my god," Audrey said. "You were with Kayla, weren't you?"

Mike laughed.

"What is so funny?"

He shrugged and tried to speak but she cut him off.

"What is wrong with you? Seriously, something must be wrong because if there wasn't, you wouldn't be doing what you're doing."

"I'm not doing anything," Mike said, corralling his laughter. "She had a lot to do at her mom's house, I was just helping out. She'll be gone come Wednesday."

Audrey leaned back in her chair and crossed her arms. Deep down, Mike knew that she knew he wasn't being entirely truthful.

"Wednesday, huh? That still leaves plenty of time for you to get into trouble."

----

36 Years Earlier

"You're going to get in trouble," Audrey said.

Dave stopped and looked back over his shoulder. "Don't be such a baby, it's just a shortcut."

"It's someone's yard," Audrey said.

Dave looked at Mike and rolled his eyes. Through the trees at the back of the yard, Mike could hear the music, could smell the smells and see the lights.

"It's not much further if we just stick to the road," she said.

"Fine." Dave rolled his eyes again. "You are such a big baby."

They turned back, walked the road for two blocks to the fairground entrance. Further in, filling the fields along the back, past the rodeo arena and show barns, was the single greatest thing to happen in a small town every summer. The carnival had arrived.

The fairgrounds sat on the edge of town, starting where Mike's neighborhood ended. Each year, he and his friends were allowed to walk over, spend the evening, and what money their parents had given them, playing games, riding rides, and eating as much junk food as they could stomach while rock music blasted from loudspeakers and the whir of generators, screaming kids, and clanking rides filled the air.

"We coulda already been here an hour ago," Dave said.

Now Audrey rolled her eyes. "An hour ago? It was two minutes, idiot."

"Don't call me an idiot, idiot."

"Would you two knock it off?" Mike said.

"Tell *her* to knock it off."

Audrey made a fist. "I'll knock it off, all right."

"Let's just go," Mike begged them.

They bought tickets and funnel cake and planned out their evening, starting with the tilt-a-whirl. They screamed and laughed each time the cart would spin enough to pin them against the back.

When the ride was over, they clanked their way down the metal steps. Dave stopped and held up a hand, a smile on his face.

"Let's ride the Ferris wheel," he said. "We can spit off of it."

He started toward the giant wheel and Mike followed, but stopped when he realized Audrey wasn't following.

"What now?" Dave asked, stopping as well.

Audrey looked from them to the top of the Ferris wheel. Mike could see she was scared. Truth be told, he was too.

"Are we going or not?" Dave asked.

Audrey looked from the Ferris wheel to Mike, her eyes pleading with him.

"Come on," Dave said to Mike. "Let's go. The big baby can wait here while we have fun."

Mike watched Dave walk away, then looked back at Audrey, still frozen in place. He wanted to stay, but he knew he had to get on that Ferris wheel or else Dave would think *he* was a big baby as well.

He turned and followed Dave, looking back over his

shoulder one last time as he went. The disappointment on Audrey's face cut him deep.

When the ride was over, Audrey was gone.

"Great," Dave said. "What a pain in the ass."

Mike's eyes widened. There were grown-ups around, someone could have overheard him.

"Let's split up," Dave said. "You go that way. Meet back here." He spun and stomped off.

As Mike strolled down the tiny midway, game runners barked out, calling to him to try his luck, it was only 50 cents a play, every play was a winner. Mike avoided eye-contact and kept walking, scanning the crowd for Audrey.

When he reached the last game booth, he had yet to see her. Maybe she was wandering around behind the midway, near the show barns. He walked around the booth and stopped when he saw Audrey and a boy he didn't recognize near one of the barns. Mike opened his mouth to call out to them, but stopped. Something wasn't right. They were yelling at each other. He couldn't make out what was being said over the music, but the tones of their voices were plain enough.

Mike wasn't sure what to do. He needed to find Dave. Dave would know.

Before he could turn, the boy pushed Audrey.

Mike froze.

Audrey pushed the boy back.

Mike watched in horror as the boy grabbed Audrey's

hair, yanked her forward as she screamed, then threw her to the ground and stood over her, yelling.

Something in Mike broke loose, something he had never felt. He charged forward, covering the distance between them faster than he had ever moved, and plowed into the kid. They landed in a heap with Mike on top and the kid flat on his back. They stared at each other in surprise for a second before the boy reached up, grabbed Mike's hair and began yanking it.

Whatever had just broken loose in Mike broke even further. Pulling hair was cheating. It went against every self-respecting boy's code of conduct when fighting. Sure, sneaking up behind a girl you thought was cute and giving her ponytail a tug just to annoy her was one thing, but what he had done to Audrey was wrong beyond anything Mike had seen. And now the kid was doing the same thing to him. Mike yelled, swung his fist and caught the boy in the nose, causing him to let go of Mike's hair and grab at his own face. It wasn't enough for Mike. In a rage, he grabbed two handfuls of hair and began slamming the boy's head into the ground, over and over. The boy wailed as Mike kept going, putting all his force behind it. He heard his name, felt something on his arm and shoulder.

It was Audrey.

"Mike, stop," she yelled over the music and the kid's cries.

Mike came to some semblance of his senses and let

go of the boy's hair. He rolled off and the boy curled into a fetal position, bawling his eyes out as he clutched the back of his head.

As Audrey helped Mike to his feet, he realized he was crying. He wiped at his eyes and nose, turned his face away, hoping she hadn't seen. The last thing he wanted was for her to think he was a crybaby.

She brushed grass from his back, then took his arm. "Let's go," she said gently, her mouth close to his ear so he could hear her.

He looked back once at the boy, still lying on the ground rubbing the back of his head, and let Audrey lead him away.

After leaving the library, Mike drove back to the house where he sat on the couch, flipped on the TV and was reminded just how bad daytime shows were. Before long, the TV was off and he was standing at the front door, holding his keys as he looked out the window. He needed to get out for a while, but was having trouble finding a reason. Except for the milk he had put off buying the day before, the shopping was done, the Jeep full of gas. He couldn't think of anyone he could drop-in on for a visit. Unless...

No, best not to overdo it.

As he stared at the outside world, he thought of the leaves piled against the front of the house and around the porch, caught there since last fall. He recalled his youth, raking leaves for his allowance, piling them in the ditch, then lighting them on fire. He could almost smell the distinct aroma now.

"Why not," he said aloud. He pushed the door open and went out, locking it behind him.

The hardware store was close enough he could have walked there in under five minutes, but he opted to drive instead. This was, after all, America. No need to burn calories when you could burn gas.

JP's Hardware was the typical small-town hardware store. The white, single-story cinder block building had been there as long as Mike could remember.

The front door was propped open, letting in the warm air and likely all manner of insects. Just inside, a man Mike guessed was in his sixties sat on a barstool behind the single cash register, a pedestal fan blowing on him.

"Hello," he said with a friendly smile. "Anything I can help you find?"

"Sure," Mike replied. "Please direct me to your finest leaf rake."

"Right this way."

Mike followed the man deeper into the store until he stopped and gestured down a side aisle. "There you go. Best rakes money can buy."

Mike eyed the two choices: One was plastic, the other metal. He lifted each one, testing its weight, unsure why he was doing so. Maybe he wanted to appear knowledgeable instead of guessing randomly or going by price alone. Whatever the case, he liked the feel of the metal rake better.

"This will do just fine," he said.

He followed the man back to the register and leaned the rake against the counter while he dug cash out of his pocket.

After paying, he made the short drive back to the house and went straight to work, ending up with a larger pile of leaves than expected. He worked them toward the street, stopping when he reached the ditch. The leaves were still damp from laying in the shadows along the foundation of the house, and Mike knew if he could get the fire started at all, it would smoke like there was no tomorrow. It might even blanket the entire neighborhood.

As he stared at the pile, weighing his options, he didn't notice the young girl walking along the road until she was even with him. She looked at him and stopped. He waved and said, "Hello, there."

"Hi," she replied. She couldn't have been more than seven or eight.

"How are you?"

She shrugged, looked past him at the house, then back to him. "Do you live here?"

"For the time being," Mike answered. "You from around here?" She had been coming from the direction of Main, two blocks over, where a convenience store sat on the other side of the street.

"We live over there," she said, pointing down the road to no house in particular.

"I see," Mike said. "You just out for a walk?"

"No, I went to the store."

Not cool, Mike thought. Where are her parents? Letting a girl that young cross a busy street by herself, then go into a store alone, in this day and age, wasn't the most fantastic of ideas.

"Why do you live here?" she asked, interrupting his judgment of her parents.

He wasn't sure if she meant the house, or the town in general. "It's just temporary, until I get things in order and find something long-term." He felt ridiculous for explaining himself to a child.

"Bradley says it's haunted."

At first, Mike wondered if he had misheard her.

"Who's Bradley?" he asked.

"My friend from school."

"Not that I'm arguing the point, but how does Bradley know that?"

"He said he saw a ghost once."

"Is that so?"

"Uh huh."

"Where did he see this ghost?"

The girl looked past him again and pointed. "There."

Even before he turned to follow her finger, a chill ran through Mike's body. He already knew what she was pointing at, but he looked over his shoulder anyway.

It was his bedroom window.

"When was this?"

The girl had lowered her hand and was kicking gently at the pavement. "Last summer. He was riding by on his bike. He said he saw someone in the window. He was gonna tell his mom on account of no one lived here. But then, just before he turned to go tell her, it disappeared."

Mike took a deep, slow breath, and exhaled. "Did he say what this ghost looked like?"

The girl pursed her lips and wrinkled her brow, deep in thought. After a moment, she nodded. "He said it was an old lady."

Mike decided against burning the leaves and left the pile in the ditch to scatter to the wind. He drove back to the library where he found Audrey sitting behind the circulation desk.

"Back already?"

"I need some help," Mike said.

Audrey grinned. "I think we all know that."

"Funny. Hey, you remember how I told you the house I'm in is haunted?"

"You mean, do I remember how you're crazy?"

"Some kid just told me that another kid saw the ghost of an old lady in the window. Now who's crazy?"

Audrey gasped, overdone and fake. "Oh my goodness. A kid told you another kid saw a ghost there? Then it must be true."

Mike sighed and crossed his arms, waited for her laughter to die down.

"I know it sounds ridiculous," he said as she got herself back under control. "But it made me wonder about the history of the place. Since I don't know how to go about tracking that down, I thought I would come drink from the fountain of knowledge."

"You've certainly come to the right place, my insane friend."

"Just tell me how."

"I'll do you one better; I know the folks at the title company. I'll see if there's an abstract I can get my hands on. I can pull the names of the previous owners from that, then research them, see what I can find. Who knows —" she leaned forward and lowered her voice "— maybe I'll find out someone was murdered in the house."

Mike didn't want to say it out loud, but that was exactly what he was hoping *wouldn't* be found. If he could be reasonably sure nothing bad had happened and that no one, especially any little old ladies, had died in the house, he would feel much better.

Audrey continued ribbing him. "You know, if someone was murdered, I bet the victim's ghost still roams the night, looking for the killer."

"I know what you're trying to do," Mike said. "You're trying to freak me out. Well, it's not going to work."

"Have you ever heard moaning or wailing late at night, by chance. That's a sure sign."

"I'm leaving now," Mike said as he stood up. He could hear Audrey's giggles as he left.

Later that day, as the world outside the living room window began to darken and the house started its usual symphony of creaking, Mike grabbed his things and headed for his Jeep. Maybe he would wander the aisles of the grocery store before getting the milk, see if something caught his eye. Kill some extra time.

He flipped on the living room light as he left, matching it to all the other lights burning in the house. It was the only one in the neighborhood with every window lit.

As he was backing down the drive, his phone dinged. He glanced at the screen and hit the brake.

Have you had dinner yet?

Mike considered his reply, went through several iterations before settling on a simple, *Not yet.*

I'm thinking of ordering a pizza. Care to join me?

After another round of careful consideration, he replied.

Sounds good. I can pick it up on the way.

The milk, after all, could wait.

They sat on the living room floor, their backs against the wall, eating pizza from the box between them.

"So," Kayla said as she grabbed a fresh slice, "what were you like in high school?"

Mike took a bite to buy himself time. He swallowed and shrugged. "I don't know. I guess I mostly tried to blend in. I didn't want to be noticed."

"So you were the wallflower type?"

"Compared to me, the wallflowers were outgoing. I tried to melt even farther into the background than that."

Kayla took a bite, the cheese stretching out between the pizza and her lips. She used her other hand to break it free, tipped her head back and dropped it in. "I'm not the most graceful pizza eater. Sorry."

"No worries," Mike said, "you're still light years ahead of me."

She grinned, wrinkling her nose as she did. "So, we never met in high school?"

Mike shook his head.

"Never bumped into each other at all?"

"Nope," he lied, hoping she might move on to another subject.

"Surely we walked past each other in the hall between classes. It was such a small school, we had to have."

"Oh, we did," Mike said. "Plenty."

He wished he had the words back as she concentrated on his face, searching her memories for one that had him in it. The last thing he wanted was to relive the night of the dance.

She continued studying his face. "I just can't recall you."

"Like I said, I blended in. Way in."

"Even so, I had to have seen you at some point."

Mike took a deep breath and let it out slowly. He looked from the almost empty pizza box to her.

"Okay," he said, "there was this one time."

Kayla sat up, crossed her legs and spun to face him. "I knew it. Tell me. Maybe I'll remember."

Mike looked at his own legs stretched out in front of him. He closed his eyes and the scene re-created in his head.

"I was leaving Mrs. Walker's history class. It was right before lunch. I was the last one out, way behind everyone else. The door was in the back corner of the room, and as I reached it, I could see a little ways down the hall. I could hear people farther down, but in the part that I could see, there was only one person. And they were walking in my direction."

"Was it me?"

He opened his eyes and nodded. "It was."

"And?"

He focused on the carpet and continued. "When I saw you, I was transfixed. You must have seen movement out of the corner of your eye because you looked over at me. And for a moment, just one glorious moment, I felt like you actually saw me. It was maybe two seconds, but it was the first time I was certain that you knew I existed." His voice was losing its strength, growing quieter with each word. He cleared his throat. "Anyway, that was it. Just a few seconds and then you looked away and passed by and was gone." He raised his head and it was like that moment all over again, only this time she didn't look away.

She blinked and the faintest smile touched her lips. "Wow. I wish I could remember that. I'm sorry."

Mike searched the room for something to stare at that wasn't her. He settled on an empty corner. "No need to apologize, it was just a few seconds out of your life that had no bearing on it whatsoever. It would be crazy if you *did* remember it."

"Maybe," she said, "but you remember."

She had him there. He certainly did remember.

"It was different for me," he said. "I was just a random underclassman. There's no reason you should have noticed enough to remember. But you —" He paused, considered stopping, but pressed on "— you were the most beautiful girl in school. Having someone like that see you, really see you, even if it's only for a few seconds, that's something worth remembering."

He risked a quick glance, saw the faint smile still on her lips.

"That's very sweet of you to say."

Mike had no response, just plucked at the carpet as the silence lingered until Kayla finally spoke.

"Was that the only time? Surely there were more."

The dance flashed through his mind, the crown on her head, Trevor walking into the bathroom, the gleaming white porcelain, the water as it dripped from his hair and the end of his nose, landing back in the bowl. And everything that came after.

"No," he lied. "Nothing worth mentioning."

The moment stretched out again until she tucked a strand of hair behind her ear and pointed to the pizza. "You want the last piece?"

"No, thanks. It's all yours."

"I really shouldn't," she said.

"But you're going to?" Mike asked, grinning as the weight of the moment slipped away.

"Oh, I'm definitely going to." She grabbed the slice and bit into it.

Mike laughed and stood up, took the pizza box to the trash can, crammed it inside, then walked back to Kayla and held his hand out. She took it and he helped her to her feet, aware of just how soft her skin was.

"It's been fun," he said, "but I should get going."

She took another bite of pizza, then held the slice out to him. "Sure you don't want even a little?"

"I appreciate the offer, but it's got cooties now."

She laughed, holding her free hand over her mouth as she chewed.

"Fine," she said, then swallowed. "I understand completely."

She followed him to the door and outside, where he turned to face her. He opened his mouth to say good night, but she spoke first.

"If you're free tomorrow evening, how about you let me treat you to dinner again at Cane's. I still owe you for all of your help. And for hanging out with me tonight." She held up the half-eaten slice. "And for paying for the pizza."

"You don't owe me anything," he said. "But I won't pass up a good a reason to get out. You may recall me mentioning the house I'm renting is straight out of the Amityville Horror."

Kayla laughed, covering her mouth again. "I think I remember you saying something about monsters in the basement."

"That and more." He kept his tone light as he pictured the unmade bed. "I also never pass up Cane's. How about I pick you up at 7:30?"

"7:30 it is."

They said goodnight and Mike left. A few minutes later, he breathed a sigh of relief. All the lights were still on.

Mike hated the grocery store on a Saturday morning. The quiet, slow pace of a weeknight was replaced by too many people and too much activity, making it difficult to relax and enjoy his time away from the house.

He went straight for the dairy section, a path that seemed counter to what everyone else was taking. He had to excuse himself several times before grabbing the milk and winding his way to the checkout line.

Waiting in line was the worst, not that he had any-where to be. Not until dinner, anyway. But the combination of the morning crawling by and the line crawling forward was maddening. He clutched the milk, listened to the beeping of the scanners and tried not to make eye contact with anyone, lest he meet someone else from his past.

The girl running the register was the polar opposite of Monotone Checkout Girl. She was cheery, friendly, and smiled a lot — all things he wasn't used to when buying milk.

After dropping the milk off at the house, he drove to the library, unsure if Audrey would be there. He was pleasantly surprised when he walked in and saw her sitting in her office, pen poised over a piece of paper.

"Hard at work on a Saturday? I admire your dedication."

He sat down across from her as she looked up and sighed.

"Trying to procure some grant money. What are you up to?"

Mike shrugged. "Nothing."

Audrey stared a moment, then laid the pen down, leaned back and crossed her arms. "Nothing? How come I don't believe you?"

Mike shrugged again. "Maybe you have trust issues?"

"Maybe. Oh, look what I have." She leaned over, pulled open a desk drawer and withdrew a thick binder. "It's the abstract on the land."

Mike leaned forward, spun it around and opened it. "Nice. You don't waste any time."

"That's why I'll be running the entire region soon. I get things done."

Mike turned a few pages, looking at numbers, names, and legal speak that didn't mean much to him, but he did recognize the name of the gentleman he was renting from.

"I haven't had time to research any of it, obviously. I'll probably get started on it Monday."

"Take your time," Mike said. "I mean, I could be murdered at any minute by whatever's lurking around in the house. This thing could provide a clue that might save me, but I don't want to impose."

"Cool beans."

"Can I borrow it until you're ready to go through it?"

"No can do," Audrey said, snatching the abstract from him and returning it to the desk drawer. "Tara is taking a risk loaning this out to me. If anything happens to it, she could get in huge trouble. I don't entirely trust you not to spill something on it, or lose it altogether."

"Fair enough," Mike conceded.

After a round of small talk and joking, Audrey walked with him to his Jeep.

"Any plans for the weekend?" she asked. "Dave just got in last night. We can hang out, watch a movie."

"Don't you guys want some time to yourselves? Isn't his next trip a long one?"

"Almost two weeks. He leaves Monday."

Dave made good money as a long-haul truck driver, but it took him away for extended periods. Audrey handled it well, but Mike knew she missed him. As much as the two used to annoy each other as kids, things had changed. Best Mike could tell, it started the night of homecoming, when Dave led her onto the dance floor.

"In that case," he said, "I'll leave you two alone. Tell him I'll catch him when he gets back."

"If you change your mind, our door's always open."

----

18 Months Earlier

Something was going on. He had ignored it, whether on purpose or not, he didn't know. It was a number of things that finally made him take notice. She began staying late at work, only here and there at first, then as many as four times in a week. He would wake up in the middle of the night, would stay still and open his eyes just enough to see her face lit by the dim glow of her phone as she tapped away on the screen. Some nights, she wasn't there at all, had slipped away to another room.

And she always, always kept her phone close, never left it laying unattended. When it finally happened, when she came in tired from a long day and wanted only to take a hot shower, Mike noticed. He had stared at the phone lying there on the coffee table, left behind for the first time in who knew how long. He had chewed his lip, realized what it would mean if he picked the damned thing up. It was a breach of trust. There would be no going back, even if there was nothing there and he never mentioned it, he would still know he hadn't trusted her enough to just ask if something was going on.

He had made his choice and easily guessed the pass-code. It was always the same, last four of her social. He opened her texts and there it was. At first, his mind had tricked him, made him think it was an accident, that she hadn't meant to send a picture showing what was show-ing. But then he had scrolled and there were more.

The entire time she was in the shower, he had scrolled. The picture count rose, he stopped to read a message here and there, but it was plain what was happening.

He kept scrolling.

And scrolling.

Two years. That's how far he made it before stopping. Two years. He had once read something about infidel-ity, about how one night could simply be a mistake, but years' worth, well, that was something altogether different.

And then Melissa had returned from her shower.

Mike tried to shake the memory, had been trying for over a year, but it would sneak up on him when he least expected. He should have been feeling good, should have been focused on dinner with Kayla, but there was the memory, tapping him on the shoulder, reminding him once again of all he had built and how it had crumbled.

He stood from the couch, walked to the kitchen and stared at the floor. The thumping hadn't returned, and he still hadn't ventured past the entrance to the base-ment. Maybe there was no need since it seemed to have stopped. Besides, old houses were quirky. That's what he told himself, anyway.

There was a lot of the house he hadn't truly explored. He mostly stuck to the living room, kitchen, and master bedroom, but there were other bedrooms, other closets and cabinets and nooks he hadn't done more than glance at.

A thought occurred to him. Perhaps there was something tucked away in a spot that had gone unnoticed for years, possibly decades. Something left behind by a previous owner, a piece of history that might tell the story of the house or its past occupants. It sometimes happened on those home renovation shows. A closer look around couldn't hurt. He hoped.

The logical place to start was as far from the basement as possible. The attic. People used to store stuff in the attic. It was a thing back then, he was fairly certain.

And on the plus side, the house's past might keep him distracted from his own.

He climbed the stairs and found what he was looking for in one of the extra bedrooms, across the hall from the master. It was tucked away in a large closet, just as he envisioned it, the pull-chain hanging from the ceiling and all.

He gave it a tug and the access door pulled open, revealing a rickety wooden ladder. Dust and the smell of age wafted down from above as he tested the rungs. Satisfied they might hold, he ascended, poking his head into the cavernous space. He couldn't see far. The attic was mostly dark, except where light leaked from under the eaves. Pulling his phone from his pocket, he turned on the flashlight app and held it up, swung it back and forth, but the light didn't carry far. He climbed the rest of the way, tested the floor with a cautious step forward. From what he could see, the attic was entirely empty, nothing but dust and rafters.

He turned back toward the ladder and looked down into the closet. Before he could start down, the house creaked, the noise coming from the back corner. He quickly aimed his light, expecting to see… he wasn't sure what he expected to see. There was nothing there, as usual. Before he lowered the light, Mike caught sight of a shape, tucked back against the slanting roof. It was square, almost invisible in its position. Were it not for the creaking, he would have missed it. Rounding the ladder, he eased his way toward it, ducked for a few steps, then dropped to his hands and knees. Despite the dim light, he could see it was a cardboard box, old and brittle, coated in dust no telling how many years deep. Carefully, he dragged it back to the access door.

He used a single finger to pull the flap open, wary of what might be nesting inside. Likely, it was full of all manner of things with four or more legs. He held the light directly over it and was surprised to find its contents in reasonable condition, no webs or anything worse.

Lying on top was a metal film canister, the kind from an old reel-to-reel projector. Under that was a smaller box that held a jumble of candlesticks and an old book of matches. He lifted them and the canister out and set them aside, revealing stacks of old photos. Pulling one out, he studied it until the house creaked again, reminding him where he was.

He dropped the photo back inside, put the candles and film canister back in, tucked the box under his arm and climbed down the steps.

The Saturday night crowd was out in force at Cane's. There had been a short wait for a table to open, but the food was still on time and perfect. Chatter and the always present smoky haze filled the air around them as they ate. The old man was back in the corner, hunched over his guitar.

"I think I'm getting used to small-town life again," Kayla said as she surveyed the room and the crowd. "Maybe I should consider moving back here."

Mike wished she wasn't joking, but assumed she was. A fella could dream, after all.

"Our little town here does have a lot to offer," he said as he picked up a fry from his plate.

"Like what?" she asked.

Mike pointed at her with the fry. "You've already seen we have a bat man, yes?"

She nodded. "Yes."

Still using the fry as a pointer, he gestured to the room around them, guitar notes wafting by, mixing with the haze and conversations. "And there's this place."

She nodded again. "Definitely a plus."

"Let's see. What else?" Mike tapped the fry on the table as he thought, and Kayla's smile widened. "Oh, we have a theater and a radio station. Granted, they don't work anymore, but still." Dropping the fry onto the edge of his plate, he laced his fingers together and leaned forward. "Are you aware we have a Walmart? One of those super ones."

Kayla placed a hand in front of her mouth as she chuckled, then lowered it. "I think we have several of those in Indy."

"Several?" Mike said, eyebrows raised. "Wow. Impressive. That is hard to compete with."

"Maybe," she said, and took a drink. Mike thought he caught a moment of something in her eye, a small break in her smile.

They talked and ate until the sun went down. Kayla grabbed the check before Mike could and paid. On the way out, the old man was packing up his guitar.

"Do you want to walk around the block again?" she asked.

Mike thought of the house and wanted to suggest they walk until sunrise.

"Sure," he said.

They reached the corner and turned left, passing by Mike's Jeep and moving down the gentle slope toward West 2nd.

Overhead, the night sky was hidden by clouds glowing

a dull orange from the town lights. Behind them, up on Main, several cars passed by.

"I wish we could see the stars," Kayla said, glancing up.

Mike didn't respond as they made the next turn.

Halfway to Broadway, Kayla nodded in the direction of the Coleman. "I wonder what the last movie was."

"Whatever it was," Mike said, "I wish I knew about it when it happened. I would have gone."

"Do you think Joe was there?"

Mike smiled at the thought and a clear image filled his head. It was Joe, his face lit by the ever-changing blue hues of ambient light from the screen, all of his attention focused on the movie, the smile that never seemed to leave him fixed firmly in place. It was an image of pure, innocent joy.

"Yeah," Mike said. "I'd like to think so."

They reached the corner and paused. "I bet he was, too," Kayla finally said. They turned away, following Broadway back to Main. Before they made the corner, Mike looked back at the Coleman. Movement caught his eye further up as the flutter of a cape disappeared into an alley.

Back at Mike's car, he clicked the fob and opened the passenger door. Kayla glanced at him, a tiny smile on her lips as she got in.

"Fingers and toes?" she asked.

Mike smiled. "Finger and toes."

The drive to her mother's house was quiet. Neither said a word until Mike pulled into the driveway and shifted into park, left the engine running and the lights on. In the passenger seat, Kayla sighed as she stared at the house.

"You okay?" Mike asked.

She nodded without looking at him. "I just don't know what to do." Her voice was barely a whisper, and Mike could tell she was talking more to herself than him. And he was sure she was talking about more than the house. He had seen it throughout the night, small flashes where her smile would drop, her forehead would crease, her attention would wander. Something was bothering her, no doubt.

He opened his door and climbed out, then walked around and opened the passenger door. He offered his hand and Kayla took it. Mike didn't want to let go once she had climbed out, but he did. After shutting the door behind her, he shoved his hands into his pockets and turned to face the house.

"You know," he said, "if you ever need to talk, about anything, you can call. Even if it's the middle of the night."

"Thanks," she said, offering a smile.

Mike studied his feet as he walked with her to the porch, waited at the bottom step as she unlocked the door and reached in to turn on the living room light.

"Thank you," she said again. "Tonight was nice."

"My pleasure, but I should be thanking you."

She hesitated before adding, "See ya," then went inside.

Mike waited until he heard the click of the lock, then turned away, climbed into his car and drove back to the house. When he pulled into the driveway, the bedroom light was off.

He closed his eyes and leaned his head on the steering wheel. Several minutes passed before he sat up and opened the door.

The rain started somewhere around midnight, hammering the old house and the entire town. Each crash of thunder shook the walls and rattled the windows to the point that Mike was afraid the place might shake apart. The flashes of lightning did nothing to make the house less spooky, instead magnifying the eeriness, creating deeper, darker shadows in the corners that took on all manner of terrifying shapes and sizes. It wasn't long before he had switched on every light.

Around one, the power went out and Mike's heart almost stopped. He fumbled for his phone on the nightstand, opened the flashlight app, and made his way downstairs to lay on the couch, close to the front door in case he decided to make a run for it. A text notification dinged as he settled in. Checking the screen, he saw a message from Kayla, sat up, and tapped to open it.

I hope I'm not waking you with this

Can't sleep with the storms, he replied.

Same here. Power's out. Is yours on? If so, I'm coming over! lol

Mike wondered how fast he could procure and wire in a generator.

It's out here too

There was a long pause before the next message came through.

Do you mind if I call?

of course not

He waited until the second ring, not wanting to appear too eager.

"Haunted Houses Unlimited, how may I direct your call?"

"I'm glad to see you're still alive. Enjoying the weather?"

Mike grinned and laid back. "Can't say that I am. You?"

"No so much. I'm not a big fan of being alone during storms. Especially when there's no power."

Mike could hear an uneasiness in her voice that conjured up the image of a young girl running into her parents room in the middle of the night, scared of the storms or the dark or both.

"Same here," he said.

"You're going to laugh, but I've been sleeping with a light on while I've been here."

He didn't laugh, didn't come close. "Yeah?"

"Yeah." She hesitated before continuing. "I don't know why. Maybe it's…"

"Hey, no need to explain."

"Thanks. I was only half joking about coming over, by the way. But, since your power is out too, and your house is haunted, I guess I'll pass."

Mike silently cursed his luck.

"Yeah, there's that." A thought struck him. "Hey, I found some old candles and a book of matches today. If you want, I can drop them by. I know it's not electricity, but it's something."

"You mean, right now?"

"Sure. I don't need them here. They would only make the place creepier, I think. And I definitely don't mind getting out of here for a few minutes."

"Okay," she said. "Sounds good."

As he stepped out, the wind swirled. The rain had eased to a sprinkle, but the air was thick and humid. Lightning flashed not far in the distance. Mike jogged to the Jeep and climbed in, tossing the box of candles onto the passenger seat. As he backed out of the drive, he glanced at the darkened house. Now that he was out, he knew he wouldn't go back inside until every light was once again burning, or daylight broke, whichever came first.

When he pulled onto Main, there wasn't a car in

sight. The streetlights were out and all the businesses he passed were dark.

When he parked behind Kayla's SUV, the front door opened and she stepped out, wearing a t-shirt and flannel pajama bottoms. Mike grabbed the candles and jogged to the porch.

"You made it," she said as lightning flashed.

"Yeah. Looks like power's out in the entire town."

"Great."

Thunder rumbled as Mike held out the box. "Here are the candles. The matches are in with them. Try not to burn the place down."

She grinned, but didn't take the box. "You want to give me a hand with them?"

"Sure." He hadn't been certain from their phone conversation if she was expecting him to come in or simply drop off the candles and leave. To be safe, he had assumed the latter. He fully expected to spend the rest of the night parked at the end of his driveway, as far from the house as possible, waiting for the power to come back on. Even then, he wasn't sure he would go back in until daylight.

Kayla used her phone to light their way inside and into the kitchen. Mike sat the box on the counter, pulled out one of the candlesticks, then stopped.

"What is it?" Kayla asked.

"I didn't really think this through. I don't have anything to put these in." He turned to her. "You don't happen to have a candelabra or two lying around, do you?"

She laughed. "No, I — Oh, wait. Mom had two glass candleholders." She spun and left the room. "I think I packed them that first day."

Mike followed her voice and found her digging through a box.

"Hold this," she said, handing him the phone. She kept digging, then moved to another box before finding what she was looking for.

"Here they are. Tada."

They went back to the kitchen and stuck a candle in each holder. Mike pulled a match from the book and struck it, holding it to each wick in turn until they were both lit. He shook the match to extinguish it just as the heat reached his fingertips.

Kayla killed the light on her phone, leaving only the candles to cast a dim orange glow into the room.

"Not bad," Mike said, looking around. When he glanced at Kayla, tiny flames danced in her eyes.

"Not bad at all," she said.

They were silent for a moment as Mike was unsure what to say. Despite being in the house, he was still uncertain if he was welcome to stay. Once again, it seemed best to err on the side of caution.

"That should keep you going until the lights come back on." He jerked his thumb toward the front room. "I guess I'll head out and leave you to it."

Before he could take a step, Kayla said, "You don't have to leave. I mean, if you want to hang out for a while, you can. I know it's the middle of the night and you probably need to get some sleep, but I'm guessing you don't want to go back to a dark house. Especially one with monsters in the basement."

Mike grinned and nodded. "You are correct. There's no way I'm going back in that house until the lights are on." He chuckled, hoping she took it as a joke, despite the fact it wasn't.

The room flashed blue and thunder rumbled. The sound of rain hitting the roof began to increase, signaling another round of storms.

"Good," she said.

They took the candles into the empty living room, sat down on the floor with their backs against the wall and the candles between them. Blue strobes of light flashed in the windows as the rain continued to pick up.

"I'm starting to think I should have kept the couch," Kayla said, drawing her legs up and wrapping her arms around them.

Mike grinned. "One would come in handy right now, that's for sure. But, you only have a few days left. I bet you can tough it out."

Kayla leaned forward, resting her chin on her knees. "Right."

The word came out soft and slow. Mike studied her a moment as she stared at the floor in front of her feet, averting his eyes to the candles when she turned to look at him.

"You know what's weird?" she asked.

"What's that?"

"When there's someone else around, storms aren't too big a deal. I mean, I still don't like them, but I don't fixate on them. But when I'm alone, I can't keep from imagining a tornado heading straight for me. I see myself buried in rubble, unable to get out, water dripping in. Or I imagine a tree crashing through the roof and trapping me under it. Or lightning hitting the house and setting it on fire." A shiver passed through her. "But when I'm with other people, I don't know, I guess it keeps me preoccupied so I don't think about those things."

Mike watched her as she shifted her gaze to the window, the soft candlelight dancing against her cheek.

She turned to him. "You probably think I'm crazy."

He shook his head. "Not at all."

"Right," she said, smiling. "You don't have to lie to me."

"Really, I get it. If I wasn't alone in the house of horrors, I probably wouldn't notice a thing. By myself, though, it's basically a living nightmare."

She laughed and leaned back against the wall, stretching her legs out. Her ponytail kept her from tilting her head back, so she removed the band, letting her hair fall to her shoulders. They stayed silent for a while, listening to the rain and thunder, and watching the candles slowly melt away.

"You know what I've been wondering?" she asked, breaking the silence.

"What's that?"

"I've been wondering what your story is."

"No story here," he said, keeping his eyes on the

candles. He didn't want her to see he was lying. The flame flickered as he focused on it and tried to block out the shadows in the room. At least here they were harmless, nothing more than what they were.

"I think you're lying."

So much for not looking. Still, he hesitated before a quick glance at her then to the carpet.

"It's nothing worth mentioning."

He hoped that would be the end of it, but it wasn't.

"There has to be a reason you moved back."

Her voice was soft, gave no hint of anything but genuine curiosity. He pulled at a strand of carpet, buying time to think.

"I hit a rough patch," he finally said. "Moving back here seemed like a good idea, a quiet place to figure things out." He folded his hands in his lap to keep from pulling a hole through the flooring. Thunder crashed outside.

"What kind of rough patch?"

Mike didn't answer, just stared from his hands to the flame and back.

"I'm sorry," she said. "I didn't mean to —"

"It's okay. Really."

The silence stretched out again until Kayla shifted, pulled her knees back up and wrapped her arms around them.

"How long do you intend to stay?" she asked.

"I guess until the lights come on, or you get tired of me and kick me out."

"Very funny," Kayla said, the small grin returning. "I meant how long do you intend to stay in town."

He knew what she had meant, of course, was just trying to dodge the subject.

It was a good question, though. How long *would* he be in town? Best he could tell, the end was still nowhere in sight.

"I don't know. I guess that's one of the things I need to figure out."

He risked a look, saw her studying him from the corner of her eye.

"Sorry if I got too personal," she said.

"Oh, no, it's fine. You're fine. You didn't get too personal. You're fine."

He took a deep breath, realizing he was on the verge of blabbering. "It's not something I'm used to talking about."

"I understand," she said. "Remember when you said I could call you anytime if I needed to talk?"

Mike nodded.

"Well, the same goes for you. If you decide you need to talk about anything, you know how to reach me."

Mike managed a weak smile and a nod. "Thanks."

They listened quietly to the rain and thunder until it dwindled to nothing, then the lights came on. Mike yawned, stretched his legs and stood up. He offered his hand and Kayla took it, pulling herself to her feet. They walked to the door, stepped out onto the porch.

"Looks like it's over," Mike said.

"Looks like it."

Mike took in a deep breath, the air scrubbed clean by the rain. "I guess I'll get going, let you get some sleep."

He stepped off the porch and was halfway to his Jeep when she called his name.

When he looked back, she said, "I hope you find whatever it is you're looking for."

He attempted a smile and climbed into his Jeep and left.

Back at the house, all the lights were on.

Mike was dreaming. He and his father rummaged through boxes, opening one, sifting through its contents, then moving it aside and opening the next.

"I know it's in here somewhere," his dad said from across the room. "I just can't remember where."

Mike dug through a box, set it aside, and pulled another one from the shelf. Opening the flap, he paused when he saw the emblem lying on top of a jumble of old screwdrivers and loose sockets.

Chevy Nova SS, written in chrome.

The emblem took Mike back to the field along a meandering dirt road that left the highway just outside of town. The fence was down where the car had gone through. Farther out, it sat in the deep grass, gleaming white and unmoving, the commotion of the aftermath long over, the authorities gone to write their reports and file them away.

"Would you look at that?" his dad said over his shoulder. Reaching inside the box, he picked up the emblem with care, raised it up toward the light. "I haven't seen this in, what, must be 30 years now. Maybe more."

Mike remembered walking the path, the grass pressed down in two parallel tracks leading to the car. He wondered what would happen to it, though that should have been the least of his concerns. For some reason he couldn't put his finger on, it felt important.

His dad had gone ahead of him, stood at the back of the car, his head down. As Mike drew nearer, taking short, slow steps, his dad slid a hand into his pocket, came out with his knife. Mike couldn't see what he did with it, just saw the knife go back in one pocket and something else go in the other. By the time Mike reached the car, his dad turned and said, "Let's go."

They didn't talk about it, Mike's family or the neighbors. At least, not where the kids could hear. The only time was at grandma and grandpa's house, his dad sat on the porch next to his own dad, shaking his head in that way that says something terrible has happened. Mike was just coming up from playing in the yard, had only caught a bit of what was being said, but as he reached the porch the conversation had stopped.

"Ol' Drew," his dad said, pulling Mike out of his

reverie. "He was a good guy. A nice guy. The world just broke him."

They studied the emblem for a moment longer, light gleaming from the polished chrome, before his dad laid it gently back in the box. Mike closed the lid, a heaviness hanging in the air, taking the wind out of their search. Still, they moved on, if at a different pace.

The dream faded before they found what they were looking for.

Mike leaned against the counter, holding a cup of coffee, and stared at the box on the kitchen table as he yawned. It had been a long night, but a good night.

He swallowed the last of the coffee and put the cup in the sink, then shuffled over to the table and sat down, pulled the box to him and opened the flap. Taking out the film canister, he ran a finger along the edge, looking for a lip to pull the two sides apart. It took some work, but it finally popped open. He wasn't sure if the reel of narrow film inside was video or audio. Unwinding a small amount and holding it up to the light was of no help.

Placing the reel aside, he pulled out photos until he had them in mostly even stacks on the table. All of them were old, many black and white, but a few featured the dull, muted tones of color film from the 70s. The adults in them were mainly stoic, posing for photos they would rather not be posing for. It was a different story for the kids, who were always smiling, looking at the camera with glee and awe.

Mike sifted through each stack, seeing certain faces recur, many across a range of ages. If he cared to put them in order, he could see them growing older, one snapshot at a time. He slowed down to admire several old cars along the way, but otherwise moved steadily forward until one black and white photo in particular caught his eye.

A man and a woman were standing side by side, him in a shirt and tie, his head topped with a fedora, her in a light-colored dress. Behind them, the frame of a building was taking a familiar shape. Mike couldn't be certain, but he suspected he was seeing the very house he was sitting in. On the back, a name was handwritten, faded from the years but still legible.

Mr. and Mrs. Horace Williams.

Mike sat the photo aside and continued through the stack until he found another of interest. The same man and woman stood in a row with three other men, all wearing suits, while three more men worked in the background. Behind them, the building was almost complete. It was definitely the house, in its final stages of construction. Not much had changed from then to now.

Mike scanned the faces of the three men standing with Mr. and Mrs. Williams, trying to recall if he had seen them in any of the other photos. None looked familiar, but it was a fourth man who caught his attention. He was among the workers in the background, pushing a wheelbarrow, obviously a member of the construction crew. Though he was caught mid-step, he wasn't looking in the direction he was moving, but instead appeared to be staring at Horace. Though his face was partially turned from the camera, there was something about his expression that struck Mike as sinister.

After checking the back, which was blank, he put the photo with the other and continued looking through the rest. When he reached the last photo, he paused. It was the house again, fully finished. This time, only Mrs. Williams occupied the foreground. Maybe it was Mike's imagination, but he thought her face betrayed a great sadness.

He put the photo aside with the other two, then placed the rest back in the box and closed the lid. After studying the three photos a moment longer, he gathered them up along with the reel, and left.

Audrey opened the door before Mike could knock.

"I thought you weren't coming by?" she asked as she stepped aside to let him in.

"I found something I'm hoping you can help with."

He held up the photos and film canister.

"Mikey!" Dave yelled from the kitchen. Mike shoved the items into Audrey's hands then braced himself as Dave ran into the room, grabbed him in a bear hug and lifted him off his feet. After two spins, Dave sat him back down. "How have you been? I thought you weren't coming by?"

"Something came up. How was the trip?"

"Uneventful. Hey, I'm making my world-famous omelet. Come have a seat."

The kitchen smelled like heaven to Mike, triggering a growling in his stomach. He and Audrey sat at the table while Dave hovered near the stove, a dishtowel hanging over his shoulder.

"So, what is this stuff?" Audrey asked, placing the photos and canister on the table.

"I was hoping you could tell me. Do you have any idea what kind of film that is and where I can find something to play it?"

Audrey popped open the canister, removed the reel and looked it over.

"Seems old. We definitely don't have anything at the library that would play it, but I think I know someone that may be able to help."

"Who?"

She replaced the film and snapped the canister back together. "Mr. Littleton. He's a retiree that comes to the library now and again looking for books on old audio and video equipment. I think he runs a repair shop out of his garage as a hobby. He's also a HAM radio enthusiast. Maybe he can point us in the right direction. Where did you get this stuff?"

"I found it in the attic."

Dave slid a chair out and sat down, the dishtowel still hanging on, the omelet left on its own for the moment. "At the house you're renting?"

Mike nodded.

"Audrey tells me it's haunted."

"It one hundred percent is," Mike said.

"It's not really haunted," Audrey groaned. "Old houses make noises, it's what they do. What's up with these photos?" She picked them up, studying each one.

"I'm guessing that's the original owners of the house. I thought it might help in tracking down info on it."

"Is that the house in the background?"

"That's it," Mike said. "There's a name on the back of one of them. Maybe it matches up to one on the abstract. Whatever the case, I thought it might help in some way."

"Good thinking." Audrey studied each photo a moment longer. "The guy is missing in this last one. And the woman looks, I don't know, sad maybe."

"My thoughts exactly."

"I'll see what I can find out about the names tomorrow."

The day progressed slowly, a lazy Sunday that was no longer different from any other day of the week now that work had dried up. To pass the time, Mike checked his bank account online, though he already knew what was there.

The account still held some reserves, enough to get by for a while, but he would need to think long term soon, maybe make a few calls, see if there were any projects he could put in for. The thought alone exhausted him, so he closed the laptop and laid down on the couch, turned on the TV, avoiding shows that he and Melissa used to watch together. When he really thought about it, that was fairly easy to do. They never had a lot in common when it came to entertainment. TV, music — none of it matched up too well. The overlapping points were few and far between and, perhaps, that disconnect reached further into their lives than he had known. But what the hell, opposites were supposed to attract, right? And they had definitely been attracted to each other, right from the start.

Even with their differences, things had been good. Surely, there had to be something else that drove a wedge between them and sent her into the arms of another man, some fundamental change, a shift in their relationship no one could have foreseen.

Or maybe the writing had been on the wall all along and he hadn't stopped to read it.

He hadn't moved in hours when his phone rang. It was Kayla.

"I hope I'm not bothering you," she said when he answered. "I was thinking about getting out for a while. Do you want to come along?"

"Sure," he replied, keeping his enthusiasm in check. "I'll come pick you up."

When he stepped outside, more of the day had slipped past him than he had realized. The sun was hanging low in the trees and the air was taking on the unique feel of evening in a small town.

Kayla was waiting on the porch when he pulled into the drive. She hopped into the passenger seat and clicked her seatbelt into place.

"I'm glad you weren't busy. I need to get away for a bit."

"Same here," he said.

She grinned. "Haunted house problems?"

"Among other things."

Downtown, the streets were quiet and mostly empty. Neither he nor Kayla had suggested going for a walk; Mike had simply parked a few doors down from Cane's and they had climbed out. They took the opposite direction than they had taken on their previous strolls. It never hurt to change things up.

"What do you remember about me from high school?" Kayla asked. "Aside from that moment in the hallway."

Mike pushed his hands into his pockets. "Hmm. Good question. I remember you drove a little blue car. I don't remember the model, but it was light blue, like an electric blue. Kind of sporty and youthful, but grown-up too. Like everything else about you."

She grinned and cocked her head. "What do you mean?"

"I just mean you seem to occupy two worlds at once. For example, you have a youthful exuberance, but at the same time a graceful, mature sophistication. You're like something that's trendy, yet timeless."

"Wow. That's a wonderful compliment."

Mike shoved his hands deeper into his pockets, stopping short of his pants pulling loose.

As they rounded the corner onto Broadway, the stoplight hanging over the intersection changed colors for no one. Up ahead, a flourishing cape disappeared into the alley.

"Looks like our local superhero is on watch."

Kayla smiled. "Should we be worried about running into someone dressed as a bat man on the streets at night?"

Mike shook his head. "Not at all. If you see anyone as a joker, on the other hand, then we should worry."

When they passed the alley, bat man was nowhere to be seen. At the end of the block, they stopped on the corner. Across the way, the Coleman stood still and dark. Mike didn't speak, only watched Kayla as she studied the marquee. When she turned to him, he looked away, hoping she hadn't caught him staring.

"Maybe we should walk over," she said, "check the doors. Who knows, maybe someone left them unlocked. We could sneak inside." A small grin crept across her face.

"And do what?" Mike asked. "Stumble around in the dark, maybe get tetanus, or break an ankle?"

"Maybe," she replied, her grin turning mischievous. "Maybe we can find the breaker, turn on the power. Who knows? The last movie might still be in the projector. We could watch it from the balcony."

The thought, no matter how absurd, set off butterflies in Mike's stomach. "That would be a dream come true."

"I know," Kayla said, becoming more excited. "The balconies were always closed. I never saw anyone up there. Wouldn't it be great to be the first in who knows how long to use them?"

Mike nodded. That wasn't what he had meant, but he wasn't going to correct her.

After looking both directions, she grabbed his hand and pulled him along. "Let's go."

He went willfully, crossing Broadway at a jog, her hand smooth as silk in his. Under the marquee, they stopped at the first set of glass doors, the ones that were always propped open at the end of the night as the theater emptied.

"Here goes," she said, smiling. At that moment, Mike swore he saw 30 years fall from her face. She was a kid again.

She pulled the door, but it didn't move. After a quick, exaggerated frown, she glided past the ticket window to the next set of doors that had been entrance-only on movie nights.

Mike followed as she paused and looked at him, a gleam in her eye. "Shall we both try at the same time?"

Her joy and enthusiasm was seeping into Mike as he took one of the handles and she took the other.

"On three. One. Two. Three."

Locked. Mike had expected nothing less. Even so,

for a brief moment, he had hoped to be wrong, that the door would pull open, the lobby would light up. On each end of the concession counter, the small windows in the swinging doors that led into the theater itself would be glowing a soft blue. They would push their way through, the houselights already out, the show already started. Down front, Joe would be staring in wonder at the screen.

"Oh well," Kayla said. "It was a fun thought."

Disappointed, they turned back the way they had come.

"I had fun tonight," she said.

They stood next to Mike's Jeep, parked in the driveway of her Mom's house.

"Me, too."

"Do you want to meet for breakfast in the morning? Or do you have to work?"

"I can get away," he said, still not caring to admit he was practically jobless. "How about I pick you up around, say, eight?"

"Eight is good. I'll be ready." She looked over her shoulder at the house and sighed. The light in the front room was on, just the way it had been when he picked her up. Mike envied her, not having to worry about the lights getting shut off while she was out. Some people had it easy, it seemed.

She turned back to him and smiled. "See you in the morning."

"See you then."

He stayed rooted to the ground, watched her stroll to the porch, up the steps, and unlock the door. Before closing it, she looked back and waved.

A few minutes later, when Mike pulled into his driveway, the light in his bedroom was off.

They sat in a booth near the front, eating and chatting as the early morning breakfast crowd thinned to nothing and the food on their plates dwindled. Mike's back was to the window that looked out onto Broadway. Kayla stared over his shoulder, watching cars pass slowly by.

"I'm going to put on weight if I'm here much longer," she said.

Mike slid his empty plate aside and leaned back, patted his stomach. "Same here. Good thing you're leaving in a few days."

The words came out with little thought, but Mike wished he had them back. He preferred not to entertain the prospect of returning to his previous existence, spending too much time in the grocery store or staring at darkened corners wondering what might pop out. Before long, Audrey would probably get the regional job, and since Dave's career wasn't dependent on where he resided, there would be nothing holding them here. They would move and then it would just be Mike and Monotone Checkout Girl, but even she was likely destined for bigger and better things.

"Are you looking forward to getting back home?"

Kayla's shrug was so slight he almost missed it.

"It's a long way back," she said.

Mike could hear the weariness in the words and was about to ask if she was all right when she looked at him and smiled.

"Are you busy tonight?"

"I'll have to check with my assistant, see if my calendar has an opening."

"Right. If there's room, I'm treating you to one more dinner as a token of my appreciation for everything you've done for me."

"There's no need —"

Kayla cut him off with a raised hand.

"Yes there is. Clear your schedule because I'm picking you up at 7:30."

"You're picking *me* up?"

"Of course," she said. "I'm handling everything. All you have to do is pretty yourself up and enjoy the evening."

Mike snorted laughter. "I'll see what I can do."

When they left the diner, bat man was standing on

the corner a block up by the stoplight, waving at cars as they passed. It was unusual for a Monday; normally he was only seen on the weekends.

Kayla waved as they drove by.

In the driveway at her mom's house, Kayla unbuckled her seatbelt and reached for the door handle.

"Don't forget — 7:30 sharp."

"I won't," Mike said as she climbed out and turned to face him.

"Text me your address."

"Will do." Mike gave a thumbs up as she closed the door and walked away.

After she disappeared inside, Mike shifted into reverse, backed out, and drove straight to the hardware store where he bought a roll of duct tape and a decent flashlight. He had an idea for later that night, one that would seem ridiculous to the casual observer, but, to him, made perfect sense. All he had to do now was kill some time. Ten hours to be exact.

For the rest of the morning, Mike alternated between staring at the unopened laptop on the coffee table and flipping through channels. At noon, he considered a trip to the library to bug Audrey as she ate lunch, maybe see if she'd had any luck with the film and the photos, but instead wandered into the kitchen and made a sandwich. He sat at the table, staring at the floor as he chewed, trying to clear his mind, not wanting to dwell on the future and hoping to forget the past. That only left the present, which, best he could tell, had come to a standstill. If he was going to make it to 7:30 without going crazy, he needed a distraction.

He finished the last bite, took a drink of water, and stood. The flashlight he had purchased earlier was still on the counter, so he grabbed it and cut open the stiff plastic packaging with a knife from the utensil drawer. After installing the included batteries, he hit the switch to test it.

Tucked away in the back corner of the kitchen was the door that opened onto the almost nonexistent backyard. There may have been a time in the house's life that it was useful, maybe a time when the backyard was larger and not encroached upon by the courthouse or overrun with unkept shrubs and trees, but that time was gone.

When Mike turned the handle, he was surprised to find it unlocked. In the time he had lived there, he hadn't once checked it, assuming it had been locked while the house stood empty, waiting on its next tenant. Also sur-prising was how easily it pulled open. The hinges made a sound somewhere between a squeak and a grind, but it was subdued, nowhere near as loud as he expected it to be. He cursed under his breath, chastising himself for being careless.

A set of three concrete steps landed him in the yard. To his right was the basement door, just as he had left it.

Switching on the flashlight, he pulled the metal door open and peered inside. Like before, the sunlight halted at the bottom of the steps, lighting up a small square of hard packed dirt floor. He took a deep breath, catching a hint of the musty air below.

The old steps were sturdy and held firm under his weight as he descended. When he stepped onto the floor, the musty smell increased tenfold.

He swept the light across the darkened space, starting high. A mix of pipes, ducts, and spiderwebs crisscrossed at head height, hanging just under the exposed floor joists. Below that, from what he could see, the space was mostly open except for multiple stone columns supporting the floor above.

When he lowered the light to the ground, he froze.

"What the..."

He took a few steps forward to get a better view. As far back as he could see, holes littered the hard packed floor. Beside each hole was a short pile of loose dirt, as though someone quickly dug a hole, left it and started the next.

Mike moved forward into the darkness, watching his footing and keeping an eye on the webs and pipes. A bump on the head was one thing, but a face full of spiders was something he wanted to avoid.

He picked his way carefully through the minefield of holes, none more than a foot or two deep, until reaching a low-hanging air conditioning duct. Beyond it were more holes. Whatever had dug them had put in a lot of time and effort doing it.

Outside of the strangeness of the holes, nothing else stuck out. There was certainly nothing that might have caused the banging he had heard. Maybe it was something simple, like one of the pipes rattling, although he knew that sound, and what he had heard that night wasn't the same.

He worked his way back toward the entrance, sweeping the flashlight from right to left. He stopped when the beam hit a brick wall in the far back corner, off to the right from the stairs. It was discolored and ragged with age, with a rough hole torn open in the center. Loose bricks scattered the ground below. The opening was the size of a manhole, the area beyond it pitch-black. As Mike moved closer, his skin crawled, and he realized he was holding his breath. He wasn't sure he wanted to see what was inside the hole, but he kept moving forward until his foot hit one of the loose bricks, sending something scurrying across the floor.

"Geez," he yelped as he jumped back, catching his foot on another brick. Flailing his arms, he tried to keep his balance but failed, sitting down hard as he dropped the flashlight. He could still hear whatever it was he sent running, moving off to his right and deeper into the darkness. He grabbed at the flashlight, fumbling before securing it, and aimed it in the direction of the noise. Whatever the thing was, it had vanished toward the front of the house.

Mike stood up, mindful of the webs and pipes, and dusted the seat of his pants. He took one last look at the brick wall and the rubble in front of it and decided he'd had enough. As he was turning away, something caught his eye. There, in the dust of the mortar from the old brick, was a single, large footprint. It looked fresh.

And it wasn't his.

Mike stepped out of the shower and grabbed a towel. After fleeing the basement, he had locked the backdoor on his way into the kitchen, then sat at the table trying to convince himself the footprint wasn't fresh after all, that it had been there a long time. It was a damp basement. There shouldn't be dust to cover it over time, right? No breeze to disturb it. And surely there was no way someone had been in his basement in the middle of the night, knocking open a hole in an old brick wall in the corner as he stood in the kitchen above, listening to the rhythmic thumping. And what was the deal with all those holes? It hadn't taken long before the feel of imaginary spiders crawling in his hair and down his shirt had driven him into the shower.

He got dressed in the bedroom then fell onto the bed, making up his mind to ask Kayla again about renting her mother's house because this place was driving him nuts.

That evening, Mike stood in the kitchen, holding the roll of duct tape. Before his trip into the basement, he had talked himself out of leaving the lights on that night, but now he was reconsidering.

Kayla would be arriving to pick him up any minute; he had to decide. On one hand, he wanted to avoid coming home to a darkened house. On the other, he didn't want Kayla to think he was a big baby, so scared of the dark that he had to leave every light in the house on. Although, if she were to witness it firsthand, maybe she would see his jokes about the house weren't really jokes at all. Maybe it would help spur a decision about renting her mom's house to him.

Or maybe she simply wouldn't notice.

He decided it didn't matter if she thought he was scared; he wasn't coming home to a dark bedroom. Not after going into the basement.

He grabbed the duct tape, ran up the stairs and stopped next to the light switch, flipped it on, tore off a piece of tape and place it over the switch. Taking a step back, he admired his handiwork, nodded and went back downstairs.

When he peeked out the front window, Kayla's SUV was pulling into the drive. He ran through the house, turning on every light on the first floor, then took a deep breath, steadied himself, and walked out.

"So this is the haunted house?" Kayla asked as he climbed into the passenger seat.

"The one and only."

Her eyes ran across it, taking it in.

"Doesn't look too creepy."

Mike buckled his seatbelt. "You should see it around 3am."

Mike had hoped to hear the guitar when he and Kayla walked in the door at Cane's, but the chair in the corner was empty. He knew it was a long shot, being a weekday, but was disappointed all the same.

The hostess led them to a table along the wall, across the room from the only other patrons. Carson appeared and made small talk as he took their orders, then left to fetch their drinks.

"Seems like a good kid," Kayla said.

"He is. I knew his mom and dad growing up. It's no surprise he's got his act together."

"I wonder what that's like," Kayla said. Mike expected a smile to follow the joke, but none came. He studied her as she turned her attention to the television on the wall and shifted in her chair. Maybe he was seeing things, but he swore something was bothering her again.

Carson returned with their drinks, told them their food would be right out, then headed off to check the other table.

Kayla turned back to him, her smile resurfacing. "I guess you're probably ready to get your life back once I'm gone. I've been taking up so much of your time."

"Definitely," Mike said, grinning. "I've been wanting to spend more evenings alone with the ghosts that haunt me." It was meant as a joke about the house, but his smile faltered as he realized it cut way deeper. "What about you?" he asked, regaining his composure. "Surely you've been missing your multiple Walmarts and working radio stations?"

"Maybe you don't realize this, but all Walmarts are pretty much the same."

"What? Get out of here."

Kayla laughed and nodded. "It's true. And with the internet, you can listen to radio stations from anywhere these days."

"Wow. You're ruining the glamour of the big city for me."

"There are harsh truths out there. You need to face them."

Mike laughed. "You sound like a friend of mine."

"This friend sounds wise."

Mike nodded and took a drink. "She is. But don't tell her that. You'll never hear the end of it."

"She?" Kayla asked, her eyebrows arching.

Mike nodded. "It's not what you're thinking. We grew up together. Same age, same class. We've been friends our whole lives."

"She went to school here?"

Mike nodded again.

"Who is it? Maybe I know her."

Mike panicked, took another drink to buy time. "I'm sure you don't," he said, setting his cup down.

Over her shoulder, Carson was coming with their food. Mike breathed a sigh of relief. He was afraid that Kayla *would* remember Audrey, would remember that night after the dance and, by extension, maybe remember him and what had happened. He didn't want her to have to relive that any more than he wanted to himself.

Carson slid their plates in front of them and Mike breathed the aroma in deep, his stomach growling.

"If there's anything you need, just let me know," Carson said, then left.

When their plates were cleaned and the offer of dessert was declined, Kayla paid the ticket and they walked out into the evening. The sun had reached the horizon to the west and the day was fading fast. Kayla stopped and looked down Main, bathed in the late-day glow.

"Wow," she said. "It's so pretty."

Mike followed her gaze and nodded. "I think photographers call this the golden hour."

Kayla pulled her phone out and snapped a picture, then slid it back in her pocket.

"Shall we go for a stroll?"

"Of course," Mike said. "The night wouldn't be complete without it."

They took their normal path counterclockwise around the block. The evening was quiet, no cars moving, the only sound coming from the slight breeze that brought with it a faint coolness. Neither spoke until they reached 2nd Street and turned toward Broadway.

"There's a question I need to ask you," Kayla said. "Something I already asked, but I want to ask again."

Mike's guard went up, mostly out of habit.

"What happened?" Kayla continued. "What caused your rough patch?"

Mike stuffed his hands in his pockets. "Technically, that's two questions." He smiled at his feeble attempt at a joke, but Kayla ignored it.

He cleared his throat, buying time to think. His instincts were telling him to deflect the question, to change the subject, but there was something in her voice, an urgency or near pleading, as though she desperately needed the answer.

"My marriage fell apart," he said, giving in. He opened his mouth to say more but found he could no longer speak.

"I'm sorry." Her voice was almost inaudible but her tone sincere.

It took a moment, but by the time they reached Broadway, Mike found his voice again. The Coleman stood quiet and dark as always on the far corner as they came to a stop.

"This town," he said, "was the only thing I felt like I had left, the only memory that was still good. That's why I'm here. I was —" He paused to search for the right words. "I don't know, dissolving into nothing, I guess you would say. I knew if I didn't do something, anything, I would just melt away."

Kayla turned to face him, but Mike couldn't bring himself to look her in the eye.

"What happened?" she asked, her voice tentative.

Mike shrugged, dug his hands back into his pockets. "A lot of things happened. A lot of things didn't happen that should have."

A single car appeared at the end of Broadway and drove slowly toward them. They both watched its headlights grow until passing them by.

"Can I ask one more thing?"

He nodded, looked down the empty street where the last of the golden light clung to the buildings.

"Who was the one that left? Who ended it?"

Mike studied the marquee of the Coleman before answering. He wished they could run across the street again, check the doors and find them open this time.

"I did."

A police cruiser turned onto Broadway a block down.

"Are you, you know, better off? Are you glad you left?"

"Once again, that's more than one question," Mike said, making another attempt to lighten the mood.

As the police cruiser crept by, Mike recognized a former classmate behind the wheel. They waved to each other and the cruiser kept going.

"I'm sorry if I'm getting too personal," Kayla said.

"It's all right. And I am. Better off, I mean. At least I think I am."

It was the first time Mike had even considered the notion and was surprised at his answer. Maybe he was making progress after all.

"Okay," he said, "my turn to ask you a question. Why do you want to know all this?"

She looked up as a nearby streetlight buzzed to life.

"Come on," she said, dismissing his question. "Let's go."

Mike decided to let it slide. She obviously didn't want to answer any questions herself, and that was fine. No need to push.

They turned back to the north but stopped when they saw a figure up ahead. Halfway to Main, bat man stood facing them in the middle of the sidewalk, his cape rippling in the breeze.

They stared at each other from a distance for a long moment before bat man turned, ran across Broadway and disappeared into an alley.

"I'm not going to lie," Kayla said, "that was the strangest thing I've seen in a while."

They both laughed and continued on, the alley empty when they passed it.

Back at Kayla's car, she unlocked the door and held it open.

"Wow," Mike said. "You weren't kidding when you said you would handle everything."

Kayla smiled and waited until he was settled in his seat.

"Fingers and toes," she said, then closed the door.

After she was situated behind the wheel, she started the engine and looked at Mike.

"I was thinking about driving around town a bit, getting a closer look at how things have changed. Do you want to come along or do you need to be getting back home?"

"My house is haunted, so..."

Kayla laughed and brushed her hair back from her face. "Say no more."

They drove and talked about places and things from their youth and how much had changed and how much had not. They circled the schools, the elementary on one side of town, the middle school and high school on the other, the old buildings now accompanied by newer, shinier ones that dwarfed the originals. Hidden in all the new, Mike could still see the old, familiar schools, tucked away but hanging on. All through town, they pointed out what businesses used to be where. The Ice Cream Churn, the Pizza Barn, the Beacon Drive-In and the former Walmarts, both of them. Western Auto, Bill's Market, the Foodliner, the old IGA. There were others that were still right where they had been all along, and Mike hoped would always be there.

As they reminisced, Mike kept seeing moments when he was certain Kayla wanted to say more but refrained. He knew something was bothering her; it was obvious even without the earlier questions.

On their second pass through town, Kayla stopped outside her mom's house. The engine of the SUV was still running as she stared at her childhood home.

"I'm going to keep it for a while," she finally said.

Mike remained cool by a narrow margin, kept from blurting out the question he wanted to ask. Hopefully, she would bring up the possibility of him renting the place without further prodding.

She shifted into gear and drove away. Neither said another word until they pulled into Mike's driveway, where he was relieved to see all the lights on. Thank goodness for duct tape.

"Dinner was great," he said. "And so was the rest. I really enjoyed it."

Kayla's lips tightened into a thin line and her eyes locked onto the steering wheel.

"Are you okay?" he asked.

She stayed focused on the wheel, barely shook her head. "I don't think I can do it."

"Do what?"

"Pretend everything is fine."

Mike could read her expression in the dim light from the dashboard.

"It's all right," he said. "You don't have to pretend. I know it must be hard losing your mom, being away from your home. It's okay to not be okay."

She stayed fixated on the wheel and whispered, "It's not just that."

"What is it?"

She took in a deep breath, held it what seemed like forever, then let it leak out.

"My husband is cheating on me."

The words crashed into Mike, causing him to flinch. He opened his mouth to say something inane, like *are you serious* or *really, that's terrible* but stopped. Instead, he asked the first substantial thing that came to mind.

"How long have you known?"

"Three weeks."

"I'm sorry."

The silence grew to an uncomfortable length before

she wiped at her eyes and looked up. "I'm sorry. I shouldn't have said anything. I'm sure the last thing you want to do is listen to my problems."

"Don't apologize. I'll listen for as long as you want."

He realized now why she had been asking questions. She was thinking of leaving and was doing reconnaissance, seeing what might lie ahead if she did, trying to pull from his experience.

Her attempted smile fell short as she wiped at her eyes again and settled back against the headrest.

"I'm such an idiot," she said. "I can't believe I didn't see it sooner."

The words were a familiar refrain. Mike had said the same things, over and over, had beat himself up to the point of exhaustion. He searched again for something to say, something more than a worthless platitude.

Before he could find the right sentiment, she raised her head and continued.

"We got married right out of college. I thought I had it all figured out. Looking back, I should have known, but I didn't. I can remember when we got engaged. I told my best friend and she just looked at me. She said, 'Are you sure you want to do this?'" She paused to take a slow breath. "I guess she saw what I didn't."

Mike felt for her. Though he didn't know *her* situation, he knew *the* situation, and he knew how much it sucked.

Somewhere deep down, he had wondered about her husband, had hoped he was a good guy who deserved someone like her, but apparently her track record in choosing men hadn't improved from high school. He would have thought, with Trevor as the starting point, she could only go up, but that didn't appear to be the case.

A realization hit him. In all the time they'd spent together, she hadn't received one phone call, not even a text. There had been complete silence and he had missed the signs, just like he had missed them with Melissa, only it hadn't been silence in that case, it had been the complete opposite. Either way, his ability to process the world around him, to read between the lines, hadn't improved.

"Things haven't been great for a long time, but I didn't think…" She paused and pinched the bridge of her nose as she squeezed her eyes shut. "What's weird is that I know there were good times, but since I found out, all I can remember are the bad. And I'm surprised by how far back it goes." She dropped her hand to her lap and stared through the windshield. "Now, I just remember all the times he was a jerk," she continued, "and how I would always defend him to my friends. I would say things like, 'That's not the real him. Underneath it all, he's a good guy.' I should have known it. All the way back to high school, I should have seen it."

"Sometimes it's —" Mike stopped, his mouth still open, as he realized what he had just heard. High school?

Kayla turned and studied him as he put the pieces together.

"What is it?" she asked.

Mike shook his head. "Nothing. I mean, I was just..."

"Just what?"

"Well," he said, "are we talking about Trevor here? Is that who you married?"

She nodded. "Yes."

"Holy crap," he said before he could stop the words from spilling out. He clamped his mouth shut.

"You too, huh? So *everyone* saw it but me. Even people I didn't know."

Mike shrugged. "I don't know about *everyone*, but..." He didn't want to tell her how he really felt about the guy.

Kayla rubbed her temple. "I was such a fool. I mean, he could be so charming and confident. I couldn't see past that."

"Hey, we all make mistakes," Mike said, still flabbergasted that they were talking about Trevor. Trevor, for God's sake.

Kayla managed a small grin. "Well, I certainly made a big one." She sighed and tucked a strand of hair behind her ear. "Sorry to dump all this on you."

"No need to apologize. I'm here for as long as you need me."

She smiled and her eyes teared up. "You're the only one I've told. How crazy is that? My husband is cheating on me and the only person I have to talk to is a complete stranger."

Mike clutched at his chest. "Ouch. Complete stranger?

What are you talking about? You and I go way back. Remember that time in the hallway at school?"

When she laughed, Mike felt good. Maybe he was terrible at dealing with problems, both his and other people's, but at the very least, if he could make her laugh, that had to count for something.

"I *don't* remember, actually," she managed to say.

"Oh, right."

When their laughter subsided, she smiled at him. "Thanks for listening."

"Anytime."

She yawned as she looked the house over again. "I should go."

"You sure?" Mike asked. "We can talk as long as you want."

"Thanks, but yeah, I'm suddenly feeling worn out. Maybe I can finally get a good night's sleep." She turned to him, an amused look on her face. "Plus, the ghosts are probably wondering where you are by now."

Mike snorted out a quick laugh. "Right. I'm sure they're worried."

He opened the door and climbed out, stuck his head back in. "Good night."

"Good night."

Inside the house, Mike felt fatigue wash over him as he fell onto the couch. It had been a long day.

He still couldn't believe Kayla had married Trevor. All along, he just assumed she had come to her senses not far into college, had found someone better, someone more like her. High school romances barely lasted past graduation, after all. He assumed hers was no different.

It wasn't fair that an asshole like Trevor got to spend so many years with someone like Kayla. The guy didn't deserve her, but Mike knew that didn't matter. Like the line from that Clint Eastwood movie: Deserve's got nothing to do with it. Still, it was a bitter pill to swallow.

Almost 20 minutes passed before he stood and climbed the stairs, not noticing the lack of creaking.

The next morning, Mike found Audrey sitting at a table in the back of the library, a laptop and the abstract open in front of her. As he approached, her fingers flew across the keyboard, then stopped when she saw him.

"Finding anything?" he asked.

"Not yet. Just getting started." She closed the laptop and propped her elbows on the table. "What brings you by?"

Mike hesitated, unsure if telling her what he had learned the previous night was a good idea. Still, he needed to talk it out with someone, so he forged ahead.

"Did you know Kayla married Trevor?"

A brief look crossed her face, like she had bitten into something foul. "Yes. Didn't you?"

Mike shook his head. "Not until recently."

"Did something happen?" she asked, now concerned. "Is he in town, too?"

"No," Mike said, cutting her off before she had a chance to get worked up. "He's not here. And nothing happened. Although, now I see why you were telling me to stay away from her." He paused for a few breaths, then continued. "She's leaving him."

"Oh my god," Audrey shouted, caught herself and lowered her voice. "You do not need to get caught up in that." She pointed a finger at him. "Whatever is going on, do not get involved."

Mike opened his mouth to speak, but Audrey pressed on. "Do not, I repeat, do not get involved. Don't offer your opinion, your advice, nothing. Stay as far away from it as you can get."

Mike sighed. "That wasn't exactly the advice I was hoping for."

Audrey stood and gathered the laptop and abstract. "Maybe not, but it's the advice you need."

Mike followed her into the workroom behind the circulation desk, where she slid the laptop and the abstract into a cabinet, shut the door, and locked it.

"Please tell me you two aren't getting friendly."

Mike made a face, hoping to convey how idiotic the thought was.

"Oh my god, you are," she said, placing her hands on her hips. "This is a bad idea. A very bad idea."

Mike shoved his hands into his pockets and shrugged. "I don't know, I guess you're right."

"I am most certainly right. There's no guessing to it." She walked away and Mike followed her into her office, sat down across the desk from her.

"You need to let this go," she said, crossing her arms and leaning back in her chair. "Nothing good can come from it. I mean, do you really think that guy has changed? I've got news for you, guys like that don't. And if she's about to go through something as painful as a divorce, which you know all about, then you know now is not the time to be getting emotionally involved with anyone or anything. Her focus has to be dealing with that." Her face softened as she uncrossed her arms and clasped her hands in her lap. "You should be focused on the same thing yourself."

"I'm already divorced," Mike said with a half-hearted grin.

"Yeah. But you're not over it yet."

----

12 Months Earlier

He didn't know how many times the phone rang that day. He'd had enough of phones. They made him sick to his stomach, made him want to move to a cabin in the woods, flee technology and all its trappings. If he hadn't been so damned tired, maybe he would have.

A knock on the door was easily ignored, but then he heard a key inserted into the lock, followed by Audrey's muffled voice.

"I'm coming in. You better have pants on."

The door cracked open and she stuck her head in, saw him lying face down on the couch, stepped in and closed the door gently behind herself.

She flipped on the light and Mike squinted, then closed his eyes and turned away.

"What are you doing?" she asked. It was a serious question, not just idle chitchat. "Ok, look. This isn't getting you anywhere. Get up right now or I will drag you off that couch."

Mike didn't move. Maybe she was serious, maybe she wasn't. Either way, he just laid there.

"Fine, you asked for it."

She grabbed his arm and yanked, rolling him over and onto the floor with a thud.

"Oh my god, I am so sorry," she said. "You okay?"

He lay on his back, looking up at her, and shook his head.

She sighed, laid down beside him, and they both stared at the ceiling for a long while.

When Audrey finally spoke, her voice was barely audible.

"You can't let what happened take everything from you, Mike. You just can't."

She reached over and took his hand in hers. "I want my friend back."

Mike opened his eyes and stared at the ceiling. The TV was still on, the volume all the way down. Outside, the world was moving along without him, the sun climbing high into the sky.

That day in the little apartment he had been renting, as bleak and gray outside as it was inside, had been a turning point for him. Maybe he didn't know it at the time, but looking back, it was plain to see. It was the following day that he had finally taken his first real step forward since leaving. He had made progress since then, though he still had ground to cover.

Audrey had always been there for him. He trusted her, loved her more than anyone, so he knew he should heed her advice because, in addition to everything else, she was wise beyond her years. He would be a fool to ignore her.

It was obvious he had let things go too far. It was time to turn the next corner.

He picked up his phone and typed out a long message, hit send as his hands were shaking, then sat back and waited.

There was still daylight left, but Mike was growing restless. It was Kayla's last full day in town and he had yet to hear from her. Maybe she needed space, a little time to process what was happening. Whatever the case, he had made up his mind he would wait for her to reach out.

Overhead, the chorus of *Day after Day* played as he waited in line at the grocery store. When it was his turn, he sat the handbasket on the counter.

"Hi, Mr. Ellerton. Did you find everything all right?"

Monotone Checkout Girl didn't wait for an answer to start scanning the few items he had picked up.

"Yeah," Mike said. "Except someone bought the last matsutake."

She raised her eyes from her work, gave him a blank stare, and kept scanning.

"It's a rare mushroom," Mike explained. "One of the most expensive foods in the world."

No response.

"It was a joke," he added.

"Are you sure?"

"Pretty sure. Because it's very rare, and we're in a small-town grocery store, which is the last place you would expect to find... You know what, never mind."

"You're total is $13.74."

He handed her his card. She scanned it and waited for the transaction to process, then gave it back to him. "Carson told me to tell you hello."

It took Mike a moment to process the statement. "Carson? The guy who works at Cane's?"

"Yes. He told me to tell you hello if I saw you."

Mike slid the card back in his wallet as she packed his items into plastic bags.

"How do you know Carson?"

"We're dating."

Mike couldn't keep his eyebrows from climbing his forehead. "Really?"

She slid the bags toward him, gave him the usual blank stare. "Yes, really. Why so surprised?"

Mike's mouth opened and closed a few times as he struggled for a way to say what he was thinking, that he had never known two more opposite people. "Well... it's just that, you know..."

"I'm way too outgoing and pretty for him?"

Mike laughed but stopped when she didn't join in.

"That's exactly what I was thinking," he finally said.

"Geez, Mr. Ellerton, stop hitting on me. I just now told you I have a boyfriend."

Mike swore he saw the corner of her mouth twitch, fighting off a grin.

"I need to find a new place to shop," he mumbled as he grabbed his bags and left.

As he was dropping the bags in the passenger seat of his Jeep, his phone dinged.

I have chocolate cake and wine to celebrate my last night here. Care to join me?

He climbed behind the wheel and started the engine, then typed out his reply.

You had me at chocolate cake. I'm on my way.

They sat on what was becoming their usual spots on the carpet, backs against the wall, a bottle of wine and a half-eaten cake between them. After the text, Mike had gone back to the house to drop off the groceries, place a fresh strip of duct tape over the bedroom switch, and turn on the living room light. He checked his phone before leaving. Still no reply to his earlier message.

"Refill?" Kayla asked.

"Maybe one more." Mike held out his glass as she poured.

"Do you mind if I ask you yet another question? And, please, feel free to say no. I won't take it personally."

"It's fine, go ahead."

"How did you find out?"

Mike didn't want to answer, but at the same time he did. Throughout the divorce, he had kept certain things to himself, confiding in no one, not even Audrey. He had never told her the details and she had never pressed him.

He took a breath and let the words flow, telling her about the pictures, the messages, and how his hand had been shaking so much he could hardly read them. It was cathartic to finally let it out. When he was finished, his glass was almost empty.

"What about you?" he asked.

Kayla took a long drink of wine, followed by a grimace. Mike wasn't sure she was going to answer, but she did.

"When I returned from the funeral, I found an earring under our bed that wasn't mine. Once I found that, the past few years started clicking into place. The late nights at the office, the disinterest, the snide comments, the snapping at me over the smallest of things, it all took on new meaning. The next morning, I checked his phone while he was in the shower, saw the same things you did, then I put it back where it was and pretended like nothing was wrong. On the way to work, I pulled over and cried in the parking lot of a Walgreens. I kept pretending for the next few weeks, then came back here to take care of the house."

It was unfathomable to Mike that she had lost her mother and then, fresh off the funeral, learned her husband was a piece of crap. He wouldn't have believed his opinion of Trevor could go any lower than it had previously been, but there it was.

"That's part of the reason I'm keeping it," she continued. "Selling my childhood home is another hit I just don't think I could take right now. And who knows, when it's all said and done, I may need a place to live."

She stretched her legs out, then pulled them back up.

"You may not believe this," she continued, "but when I was driving down here, I had basically made up my mind to just keep pretending and see what happened. I was so scared. I mean, we've been together for so long. I can't remember a time when we weren't. I was more than scared, I was terrified, but as miserable as I was feeling, the thought of being alone scared me even more. I just didn't think I could bring myself to confront him, to end things."

She paused and looked at Mike, a half-smile touching her lips.

"Then I met you, and I realized something. I began to see I wasn't alone. I knew you had gone through something yourself, even though I didn't know exactly what it was. I finally started asking those questions because I needed to know..." She trailed off, shrugged and sighed. "I guess it was comforting to know there was someone else out there going through the same thing. That sounds bad, doesn't it?"

"No. I get it," Mike said. "All of it."

Neither spoke for a while as they finished the last of the wine. Kayla got up and threw the bottle into a trash bag hanging from the pantry door, then returned with two bottles of water.

"So you've decided not to ignore it?" Mike asked.

She nodded. "Yes."

"That's good. He doesn't deserve you. He never did."

She eyed him sideways and smiled. "Thanks. I wish I could take you with me for support."

Mike barked out a short laugh. "I doubt that would go over well. Besides, I'm sure you have friends that will be there for you. You don't need me."

She traced her finger around an indention in the carpet.

"My friends stopped coming around a long time ago," she said, a deep sadness in her voice. "Only one ever came right out and said it, but they didn't like Trevor. His friends became my only friends, and I'm pretty sure whose side they'll land on."

Mike thought for a moment as he watched her finger still tracing the carpet.

"I think you might be surprised," he finally said. "I bet your old friends will resurface the moment they find out. I bet they miss you and will come running back to support you."

"Maybe," she said. "Maybe."

Mike tapped her gently on the knee to grab her attention away from the carpet. "Hey, if at any time you feel alone in this, just give me a call."

Her smile widened. "I will."

"Good." He leaned his head back against the wall with a thud. "You really should have kept the couch."

They both laughed, picking up steam until they couldn't breathe and had tears in their eyes.

After catching her breath, Kayla asked, "What was the worst part for you?"

Mike let his smile fade as he thought.

"There were two worst parts," he said. "The first time I saw the messages." He rubbed at his cheek and took a deep breath. "Seeing the things she was saying to someone else…" He trailed off, but picked back up after a few moments. "And then there was the fact that my entire life changed. Because she kept the house, I lost the home I had known for 15 years. I went from a familiar, comfortable place and always having someone around to being alone in a strange apartment. My surroundings changed, my routine changed, my whole thought process just… changed. There was nothing familiar left. That's why I wound up here." He pulled at the carpet to occupy his hands. "What about you? What's the worst part so far?"

"So far, I think the worst thing is feeling like a failure.

Like it was somehow my fault, that I didn't do enough to keep him interested, that I failed at being a wife."

The answer surprised Mike as it drilled into him. God knows he had felt the same at times.

"If you think you're a failure," he said, "you've got it all wrong. You're not a failure. I'm not sure I've ever met someone farther from it."

She laughed and wiped at her eye at the same time.

"Thank you," she said. "I have one more question."

Mike groaned as he smiled. "You always say that, and it's always more than one."

"I mean it this time. Maybe."

"Fine, go ahead."

"How long do you think it will be?"

"How long will what be?"

"How long before you try it all again?"

It was something he had been contemplating from the start. How long before he would be ready to date again? He had assumed the biggest hurdle would simply be finding someone. He had to face it: most women his age were taken, settled into roles in families they had been building for years. The ones that weren't taken, well, there were usually reasons why. He knew the chances of finding someone who would also find him were slim to none. With no children and a shallow pool of potential mates to draw from, the frightening prospect of dying alone was all too possible. So possible that he preferred not to think about it, and yet he had.

And then Kayla appeared. The only problem was that

she had to go through her own changes, and that could take time. And who knew if she even felt anything toward him besides friendship. And there was the fact she would be 700 miles away. Anything substantial was a pipe dream, of course, but it was nice to pretend. He knew the likely outcome was they would keep in touch for a while as she sorted out her life and where it would be going next. And then the calls and texts would come in less and less until one day they stopped altogether.

"I don't know for sure," he said. "I guess it depends on finding the right person. And letting go of the last one."

Kayla looked up, then back to the carpet, pulled at the fiber again. "You haven't let go yet?"

"I'm working on it."

Outside, the night was cool and still. They stood on the porch, neither wanting to be the first to end the night. The silence grew awkward until Kayla broke it.

"Will you come say goodbye tomorrow?"

"Of course."

"Good. I won't leave until noon. I don't want to drive the entire way in one day, so I'll break it up over two, maybe three."

"Sounds like a smart plan."

The silence stretched out again, and this time Mike ended it.

"I should get going, let you get some sleep."

Kayla nodded and followed him to his Jeep.

"How about I come with you?" she asked. "I don't

know if I can spend another night here alone. Especially with it being so empty now."

Mike's heart thumped in his chest even though he thought she was joking.

"Sure," he said. "As long you don't mind things going bump in the night."

She eyed him sideways and grinned.

"That's not what I meant," he added with a laugh. "Get your mind out of the gutter."

She laughed as well and tucked her hair behind her ear. "Right. Your house is haunted."

"Exactly."

"You know, it may be the wine talking, but I think seeing a ghost would be pretty cool."

The way she smiled at him told Mike she wasn't joking after all. His heart skipped a beat, but he quickly composed himself.

"It's definitely the wine talking," he said with another laugh, hoping this one didn't sound forced.

She frowned and nodded. "I guess. See you tomorrow?"

"See you tomorrow."

As Mike backed out of the drive, he cursed the voice in his head. If it hadn't been for it, he would have opened the passenger door for her, motioned her in, but that voice, Audrey's voice, was screaming at him to not be an idiot. She was going through a tough time and she had some wine in her. As much as it pained him, the last thing Mike wanted was to be part of something she would regret come morning.

He made the short drive to the house and, when he pulled into the drive, the bedroom light was still on. He killed the engine but stayed in the Jeep, racking his brain. Leaving the lights on had become routine, a habit he no longer thought about, especially when it came to the bedroom. But the living room, that one hadn't been an issue so far. It had always stayed how he left it. The bedroom had been the only problem.

Until now.

Taking a deep breath, Mike forced himself out of the Jeep. Not only was the night air dead still, but an ominous quiet had settled over the town. No cars, no trucks passing by over on Main, no leaves rustling in the trees, nothing. Mike could hear the grass swishing underfoot with each step. When he reached the porch, he kept his eyes on the doorknob, afraid to look in the windows for fear of seeing something looking back.

After fumbling with his keys, he managed to get the right one into the lock, but he didn't turn it right away. He needed a moment to steady himself, to tell himself he was being ridiculous, just as he had done a thousand times since moving in.

He realized he wasn't breathing and forced air in and out of his lungs before biting the bullet and turning the lock. Pushing the door open, he stood on the threshold and peered into pitch black. Every muscle in his body tensed as he quit breathing again, felt for the light switch just inside the door, found it and flipped it.

Nothing.

He tried the other direction. Still nothing.

The light must have burnt out. It was at once a relief and a problem. Relief because it meant something hadn't come along and switched it off; a problem because now he had to walk into the darkened house, through the living room and into the kitchen, where he would find the next closest light. He knew for certain he had been lax and left the kitchen light off, so with any luck, it was still working.

He pulled his phone from his pocket, turned on the flashlight, and took a deep breath to steady his hand.

The light cast shadows in the room, somehow making things worse. He shook his head, reached in and pulled the door closed, returned to his Jeep and climbed in. The house loomed in front of him as he tossed his phone on the passenger seat, then leaned his own seat back. It would be a long night.

Something woke him; whether it was his back aching and his butt going numb from sleeping in one position, or a truck passing by on Main, he had no idea. He rubbed at his eyes and raised his head, looked over the steering wheel, through the windshield that needed cleaning, to the house. The bedroom light was off.

"You've got to be kidding me," he mumbled.

He checked his phone for the time, groaned when he saw it was barely past three. A lot of night still lay ahead, and the thought of spending it in the Jeep was not a pleasant one.

He yanked the lever to bring the seat back upright, reached for the door handle to step out for a quick stretch, but froze when he saw something move behind the house. A dark figure slipped past an opening in the bushes at the back corner, heading toward the courthouse, a figure with pointed ears and a cape.

"What the…"

Mike watched as bat man reached the courthouse, turned north, and disappeared from view.

First, bat man had appeared on his walks with Kayla. Now, he was lurking around the back of Mike's house. And if he had been lurking around the house, maybe he had gone into the unlocked basement. Maybe he was the source of the footprint, a fact which should have concerned Mike more than it did, but was actually a small relief. At least with bat man, he knew what he was getting.

Bypassing the urge to get out and stretch, he leaned his seat back and settled in as best he could, images of superheroes stuck in his head.

Mike woke early, every part of him aching. The sun wasn't visible above the trees and buildings yet, but there was plenty of light. He grabbed his phone and stumbled into the house, fell on the couch and was dozing when a new notification sounded. He stared at the message a long time. Three simple words.

I'd like that.

After a long sigh, he replied.

See you this evening

Shortly before noon, Mike drove to the library, walked into Audrey's office, and closed the door.

"You were right," he said, taking a seat.

"Of course I was." Her eyes stayed glued to the computer monitor perched on the corner of her desk. "About what?"

"I still have work to do."

She stopped what she was doing and focused her attention on him.

"I decided to face it head on," Mike continued, "not run away anymore."

"That sounds promising."

"Yeah. It also scares the crap out of me."

She smiled, warm and comforting. "I know, but you're going to be all right."

"I'm glad one of us thinks so."

"I don't just think so, I know so."

Her confidence in him was always there and was always reassuring, even when he lacked it himself.

He stood and pulled his keys from his pocket. "Anyway, I just wanted to stop by and tell you."

"Leaving so soon? You just got here."

"Yeah, I told Kayla I would stop by before she left, say goodbye."

Audrey visibly tensed. Mike raised a hand to cut her off before she could lecture him.

"I know what you're thinking, but I assure you I didn't do anything stupid. And won't do anything stupid. At least, not anytime soon."

"Good," she said, relaxing. "Come on, I'll walk you out. Oh, by the way, Mr. Littleton has a player for that tape reel. He's bringing it by around four to show me how it works and let me borrow it for the night. How about you come by and we'll have a listening party?"

"Sounds good, but there's something I need to take care of first. I should be back in town around 7:30 or so. Would that work?"

"Sure, but if I have to stay up late and this tape turns out to be nothing but boring drivel, or worse, blank, you will never hear the end of it."

"I know," Mike said. "I'll get here as soon as I can."

"You better."

The back hatch of Kayla's SUV was open, revealing a wall of cardboard boxes. Mike parked and climbed out of his Jeep just as she appeared on the porch. She waved to him and he waved back.

"Perfect timing," she said as he neared. "I'm down to the trunk in the bedroom. Can you give me a hand with it?"

He followed her inside where they each grabbed an end and lugged the trunkful of memories outside. There was just enough room to slide it against the stack of boxes and close the hatch.

Back inside, Kayla took one last look through each room, making sure nothing was missed. All that was left were the beds in both the master bedroom and her old room, along with their accompanying nightstands. Aside from that and the appliances in the kitchen, the rest of the house was empty.

"I guess that's it," Kayla said, her voice quiet as she looked one last time at the living room before switching off the light. Mike led the way out, waited on the porch until she had closed and locked the door.

They walked without speaking to her SUV, where Kayla pulled a single key from her pocket and held it out. "I know I've been asking a lot of you, but would you mind keeping an eye on the place for me?"

"Of course, no problem."

Mike held out his hand and she placed the key in it.

"I'm leaving the power and water on until I know what's going to happen. But, once things are sorted out, I like the idea of you renting it."

It should have been good news for Mike, but it fell flat. Him moving in only meant she wouldn't be. He would much rather stay in the house of horrors than see her leave.

"Thanks again for all your help." Her smile was subtle and beautiful, so much so that Mike had to look away.

"My pleasure," he said, studying his feet.

Kayla stepped forward and they hugged for a long moment, then Mike opened the door for her.

"Be careful on the drive," he said. "And keep me posted."

She nodded and situated herself behind the wheel.

"Fingers and toes," he said as she smiled and showed him her hands.

After starting the engine, Kayla rolled down the window.

"I know this sounds weird, but I'm going to miss dinners at Cane's, the walks through town, and staying up late talking."

A jumble of thoughts fought their way up for air, but Mike pushed them all back down.

"Same here," he said.

She smiled one last time, then shifted into gear and backed away.

Mike thought the hour and a half drive to his former home would feel like an eternity, but he had been wrong. It passed in the blink of an eye.

Pulling into the drive that he had pulled into a thousand times before was familiar and foreign at once. Seeing the yard, the house, the walkway from the garage to the front porch, was like an out-of-body experience, like he was there and yet not.

When he knocked on the door, the familiar bark of his old friend Sheeba sounded from inside. Melissa answered and Mike sank to his knees as Sheeba crashed her large furry body into him, licking his face while her tail beat so fast it threatened to destroy anything in its path. He hugged her as she shook with excitement, reduced to a puppy again, squirming with unbridled joy. Tears filled Mike's eyes.

"Hey, old girl," Mike said. "I've missed you."

The day he had left, he wanted to take her with him, but he had no idea where he was going. When he eventually found an apartment, it wouldn't allow pets, otherwise he would have returned for her. Instead, he had to leave her behind, which was one of the toughest parts of it all. By the time he rented the house, he had come to realize that ripping her away from the only home she had ever known might not be for the best.

Melissa waited patiently in the doorway until Mike finally stood and Sheeba sat on his feet, leaning against him as she fidgeted nonstop.

"I haven't seen her that excited in a while. She misses you."

Mike nodded and rubbed Sheeba's ears, unable to speak yet.

"Come on in," Melissa said, standing aside.

They sat at the kitchen table, Sheeba at Mike's side, panting, her head resting on his leg as he continued rubbing her ears.

"I'm glad you texted," Melissa said. "For a while now, I've been wanting to get in touch. There are some things I need to say and I've —"

"If you don't mind," Mike cut in, "I'd like to say what I have to say and then leave." Melissa's mouth hung open, then moved without making a sound until she closed it and nodded.

"I want you to know I don't blame you and I don't hate you," he said. "I missed a lot of things, and I'm sorry for that. I don't like what you did, I never will, but I understand."

Melissa moved to speak but Mike pressed forward.

"Sometimes things aren't working and we don't see

it until something happens that opens our eyes, or until someone comes along and holds a mirror up and we suddenly see what we couldn't before." He took a deep breath and let it go. "We both made mistakes. They shouldn't define us. I hope you find what you're looking for and I wish you all the best."

He gave Sheeba a pat on the head and stood. "I have one request."

"What's that?" Melissa asked, her voice cracking.

"Can I visit Sheeba now and then?"

She smiled and nodded. "Of course."

"Good."

Mike knelt and gave Sheeba another bear hug, then left.

Audrey carried two plates of lasagna into the room and sat them on the coffee table next to the reel-to-reel tape deck. An extension cord ran from the worn device to an outlet across the room, the reel already loaded and ready to go.

"What was it you had to do earlier?" she asked as she sat down next to Mike on the couch.

"Hmmm?" he asked, reaching for a plate. He heard the question, was only pretending otherwise.

"You said you had something to take care of. What was it? And I know I'm being nosy, so no need to point it out."

"Oh, that," he said. "I went to see an old friend."

He took a bite of lasagna, expected Audrey to ask who

the old friend was, but she didn't. She stared at him, un-moving, a single eyebrow raised, then asked, "And how is Sheeba?"

Mike couldn't help but chuckle. She had always been good at reading him.

"She's all right."

"And?"

"And," he continued, "I took the first truly meaning-ful step forward that I've taken in a while."

"You don't know how good that is to hear," she said, getting up and leaving the room.

Mike heard the refrigerator door open and close, fol-lowed by a cabinet door. When Audrey returned, she was carrying a bottle of wine and two long stemmed wine glasses.

"This calls for a toast."

Mike took the wine and popped the cork, filled each glass halfway.

"To letting go and moving on," Audrey said, raising her glass.

The tape started slow. The voices coming from the tiny speaker were muffled and distant, and as the sec-onds ticked by, Mike worried the entire thing would be that way. Then the clearing of a throat sounded, loud and strong, followed by the bang of what could only be a gavel.

"Let's get started, gentlemen, if you please."

"This hearing concerns rightful ownership of lot 25. I have here the deed to the land, showing ownership by a Mr. Charles Williams. Mr. Williams, as I understand it, passed away recently. Is that correct?"

"That is correct, Your Honor."

"And you are Mr. Williams' son, correct?"

"Yes, Your Honor. Horace Williams."

"I am also given to understand that the land in question is currently occupied by one Anson Krebs. Is that you, sir?"

"That'd be me."

"Please address the court appropriately, sir."

"That'd be me, Your Honor."

"Mr. Williams, did your father have a will?"

"No, Your Honor, he did not."

"What about your mother?"

"None as well, Your Honor. She passed 3 years ago."

"I'm sorry for your loss. Mr. Krebs, you are claiming the land in question should belong to you. Please explain."

"I ain't claiming it. I'm telling you flat out that Charles gave me that land to tend."

"Your Honor, if I may —"

"You may not. I'll come back to you in a moment. Now, Mr. Kreb's, what do you mean, Mr. Williams *gave* you the land."

"I mean just that."

"You'll have to pardon my confusion, but why would he simply give away a plot of land?"

"Charles and I known each other our whole lives. We fought in the Great War together. Made it out alive. When that mess was over, I came back home, farmed on land owned by my family, out west of town. When the Depression came, the bank came with it. They took what little I had. That's when Charles let me take over that plot of his land. Said it wasn't much but I could live out my years there, if'n I wanted to, and I reckon I do. Said it was mine as long as I wanted it."

"And did you pay him for the land?"

"He didn't want no money for it."

"Mr. Krebs, do you have any type of document that would support your claim to this land?"

"Ain't no documents. We had a deal on a handshake. That's all I need."

"Unfortunately, Mr. Krebs, the court needs more. Is there anyone that can bear witness to the fact Mr. Williams and yourself struck such a deal?"

"There ain't."

"I see. And Mr. Horace Williams, as Charles Williams' son, you wish to take control of the land, correct?"

"Yes, Your Honor. My Wife and I wish to build a house, raise a family."

"Build your damn house elsewhere, you got plenty of land."

"Mr. Krebs —"

"I got a right to that land."

"Mr. Krebs, you will address me and only me. Understood? I will not tolerate those types of outbursts. Now, where were we? Mr. Williams, you wish to build a house on the land owned by your father, correct?"

"Yes, Your Honor. I informed Mr. Krebs of my intentions and asked that he find another place of residence in a reasonable amount of time."

"Reasonable my ass."

"Mr. Krebs! You will remain quiet until spoken to. Do you understand? Now, once again, let me make certain I have this straight. Mr. Williams, are you the sole heir of your father's estate?"

"Yes, Your Honor. I have no brothers or sisters."

"And no other parties, besides Mr. Krebs, can claim any interest of ownership?"

"That is correct, Your Honor."

"Mr. Krebs. How long have you lived on the land?"

"Seven years."

"What date did you first occupy that land?"

"February 19th. 1930."

"I wish to disagree, Your Honor."

"One moment, please. Mr. Krebs, do you have any documents or witnesses that can corroborate that date?"

"I ain't."

"Mr. Williams, why do you disagree?"

"He disagrees because he's a damn liar."

"Mr. Krebs, this is your last warning. One more outburst and I will have you held in contempt and removed from this hearing."

"Your Honor, if I may. It is my opinion that Mr. Krebs is not being truthful about the date so that he may claim adverse possession. I notified Mr. Krebs of the passing of my father and my imminent inheritance of the land on February 24th of this year. He shifted the date of his arrival to the land simply to meet the seven-year requirement. In fact, he did not take up residence on the land until May of 1930."

"That's a damn lie and you know it!"

"Order, please!"

"I ain't listening to these lies. That land is rightfully mine. The only way I'm leaving it is dead."

"Mr. Krebs, control yourself!"

"You come try to take it. Any of you. I'll be damned if I go without a fight."

"Mr. Krebs. Sit down immediately!"

The voices blended in a din of shouting as the gavel banged. After a loud, dull thump, the tape went quiet.

Mike and Audrey looked at each other, eyes wide.

"What the..." Mike said, his voice trailing off for a moment. "Do you think they're talking about the land the house is on?"

Audrey nodded. "I *know* they are. I recognized the names of Charles and Horace from the abstract."

Mike sank back into the couch and turned it over in his head. "What about the other guy? Krebs?"

"Didn't ring a bell. He certainly never gained ownership, that much I do know."

Mike looked at the player, the reel still turning. "There's still a lot of tape left. Maybe there's more."

"Let's find out."

Audrey sat up on the edge of the couch and worked the player, fast forwarding the tape a moment, then playing a moment, scanning for more audio. As she searched, Mike grabbed the empty glasses and half empty wine bottle and took them to the kitchen. When he returned, he sat on the couch and watched the reel dwindle to nothing.

"That's it," Audrey said as the last of the tape fed through the head and began flapping on the reel. She hit stop.

Mike sighed. "So I'm guessing the house that Horace was wanting to build is the house I currently live in."

"Probably. It's an old house. The time frames most likely line up."

Mike nodded and rubbed his chin. "I wonder if Krebs went quietly or if he kept his promise." A thought pushed its way to the front of his mind. "I wonder if that was Krebs in the photo. The guy pushing the wheelbarrow who was staring daggers at the others."

Audrey thought it over. "Why would he be there? From the sound of it, he didn't like Horace at all. I can't imagine he would help Horace build a house on what he thought was his land."

"Whoever it was, he wasn't happy to be there."

"True. But Krebs said he was in the Great War with Charles. That would make Krebs much older than Horace. The guy in that picture didn't look older, did he?"

Mike closed his eyes and pulled up the image in his head.

"I don't think so," he said, then stood and stretched his lower back. "Whatever the case, it would be interesting to know who that guy is."

"Well, you're in luck," Audrey said with a grin. "You happen to know the best researcher in the tri-county area."

"Do I? Who?"

She stood and slapped him on the arm.

"Wait a minute," Mike said. "Is it you? It's you, isn't it?"

Audrey pointed to the door. "Get out of my house."

"Fine. I'll just go back to my place, where the ghost

of Anson Krebs has probably turned off all the lights by now."

Ringing woke Mike. Light was already streaming into the room, forcing him to squint as he felt along the bedside table until his hand landed on his phone.

He tried to read the caller ID on the screen, but his vision was still blurry from sleep. He hit the answer icon, which was nothing more than a green smudge, and put the phone to his ear.

"Hello."

"Hi," Audrey said. "You sound terrible. Did I wake you?"

"Yes. What's up?"

"I found something."

Mike rubbed at his eyes with his free hand, trying to clear his vision.

"You what?"

"I found something."

Mike blinked as the room came slowly into focus. He gave it a quick once-over to make sure nothing had happened while he slept.

"What are you talking about?" he asked.

He heard a sigh and pictured her rolling her eyes.

"The house," she said. "I found something."

He sat up and swung his legs over the edge. "Already? What is it?"

There was a pause before she answered.

"I think you better come down here."

The entire time he was showering and dressing, then making the short drive to the library, Mike felt uneasy. The fact that Audrey wouldn't tell him over the phone what she had found could only be bad.

The library had been open for half an hour when he pushed his way through the glass doors. He scanned the room and found Audrey sitting at a table in the back, bent over an open laptop. After saying a quick hello to the ladies at the circulation desk, he made his way to her.

"You didn't waste any time," he said, pulling out a chair and sitting across from her.

She didn't look up from the screen. "Couldn't sleep. I came down here about three this morning and starting searching. I wanted to find out more about Anson Krebs."

Mike yawned, and settled back in the chair. "Anything good?"

"Not good, no," Audrey said. "In fact, it's pretty much all bad."

The news didn't surprise Mike; he had expected as much.

"Anson Krebs died before anything was officially decided on the land," Audrey said. "My guess is, it wasn't long after the hearing. Doesn't matter, though. The point is, with no more claims to the land, it was legally passed to Horace. But what *does* matter is that Anson Krebs had a son, and the son had a run-in with Horace not long after. He was arrested on aggravated assault charges."

She stopped to take a breath and turn the laptop around. On the screen was a black and white mugshot of a rough-looking man with dark hair and even darker eyes that looked familiar, though Mike couldn't place him.

"Is that Anson's son?" Mike asked.

"No, but we'll get to him in a moment." Audrey paused and took a breath. "As it turns out, Horace was murdered."

"By who? Anson's son?"

Audrey shook her head. "Nope."

"By this guy?" Mike said, pointing to the screen.

Audrey nodded. "Yep. While Anson's son, whose name is Royce Krebs, was in jail for the assault, he started talking to a man in the cell next to his. Turns out, Royce really liked to talk. He ended up telling the man how he had landed in jail. That man was also in for assault and petty theft, and Royce told him all about how his father had his land stolen away from him and how he had died of a heart attack before getting what was rightfully his. And he told him about how he went to find the money he knew his father had stashed away in the cellar of his shack. And not just money. Royce thought he had gold squirreled away as well. Royce was convinced his father had smuggled it back from the war. The only problem was that Horace showed up before he could find it and they got into an argument, then punches were thrown and that's what landed Royce in jail. But he told the guy in the cell next to him that as soon as he got out, he was going after the money again and nothing would stop him."

Mike held up a finger. "How do you know all of this?"

"It all came out in a trial later on."

"A trial for what? The assault?"

Audrey shook her head. "Nope. I'm getting to that. What happened was that Royce and the man in the cell next to him decided to work together to find the money. When they were both released, Horace had already started work on the house. The shack had already been razed, but there was a cellar that was incorporated into the basement of the new house. The man in the cell got hired on to the construction crew. The plan was to search for the money any chances he got. Then, once he located it, he and Royce would sneak back in at night, split the money and run."

Mike interrupted with a laugh. "Why do I get the feeling this plan blows up?"

"Because it does," Audrey said. "The man decides he's going to find the money and keep it all for himself. The house is close to completion and he hasn't found anything. So, he sneaks in one night, determined to find something, but just like with Royce, Horace shows up. The man kills Horace with a hammer and flees."

Mike flinched as he realized why Horace wasn't in the third picture of the house and why Mrs. Williams looked so sad. And then something else clicked. The second picture, the one with the man pushing the wheelbarrow, staring at Horace. Mike would have to compare the two closer, but he was willing to bet the mugshot on Audrey's screen would share more than a passing resemblance with the staring man.

"He's picked up a few weeks later," Audrey continued. "He tells the cops everything and implicates Royce, who is also arrested. The two are convicted of murder and accessory to murder and spend the rest of their lives in jail. For Royce, that wasn't very long because he hung himself with a bedsheet after two years."

"Geez," Mike said. "What a train wreck."

Audrey took a deep breath. "Here's the part you may not want to hear," she said. "Horace's wife lived out the rest of her years in that house. She never remarried."

"Why would I not want to hear that? What, was she murdered too?"

"No, she passed away from natural causes. But, the thing is, she passed away in the house. In her bed."

Mike's mind spun for a moment, then stopped on the

bedroom. He thought of the unmade bed and the kid who was too young to be crossing busy streets on her own, the one that had relayed Bradley's story about an old lady in the window. A shiver ran down his spine.

Audrey must have seen the look on his face because she winced as she spoke again.

"It gets worse."

Mike pinched the bridge of his nose and closed his eyes. "Great. What else?"

"The other day, you remember how I was joking that maybe someone was murdered in the house?"

"Yes," he said, drawing the word out. He had a bad feeling.

"Well, I wasn't wrong. Horace was killed in the kitchen."

"Holy shit," Mike said, far too loud. He clamped a hand over his mouth and surveyed the room. No one else had come in yet; only the ladies at the desk stared back at him. He turned back to Audrey and lowered his voice.

"You mean I've been living in a house where an old lady died in her bed, probably in the very spot I've been sleeping, and a guy was murdered in the kitchen?"

Audrey shrugged, a pained look on her face. "Sorry."

He had definitely wanted to know the history of the house, but now that he knew, he wished he didn't. He realized he could never go back to just thinking the house was old and creaky. Now, every sound would be coming from the ghost of a murdered man or his long-suffering wife.

"Well, that's that," he said. "I'm moving out."

Audrey forced a smile. "Anyway, I would be willing to bet the murderer, whose name is Jeb Martin, is the man pushing the wheelbarrow in the photo." She pointed again to the laptop screen. "This guy right here."

"Great minds think alike," Mike said, nodding.

When Mike returned to the house, he sat in his Jeep a long while, studying the exterior and turning its secrets over in his head. When he finally climbed out, he walked into the yard, searching for the right angle until he was sure he was standing on the spot where the second picture had been taken.

Forcing his feet to move, he went inside, grabbed the photos, and sat down at the kitchen table. Using his phone, he snapped a picture of the second one, then pulled it up and zoomed in on the wheelbarrow man. Though half his face was turned from the camera, there was no mistaking it was the same man whose mugshot Audrey had found. It was Royce's accomplice, Jeb Martin, after being hired but before the night he had returned to the house after dark, looking for the money that was supposedly there. Mike had no idea what the man had found, if anything, but whatever happened, the end result was murder. Mike looked up from his phone and studied the kitchen floor, as though he might be able to see the very spot where Horace had left this world. He wondered if Horace's wife had found him, had maybe gone looking for him when he hadn't returned home.

He could envision it, Horace lying face down, a dark red pool around his head, a bloodied hammer nearby on the floor, his wife walking into the room, stopping and screaming, then falling to her knees, weeping hysterically. Then again, if she had been the one to find him, how could she have gone on to live in the house? Maybe someone else had discovered the grisly scene and Mrs. Williams had been spared the horror. And maybe she lived out the remainder of her years in the house because it reminded her of her husband.

A shiver ran through Mike as he shook the thoughts away. After checking the backdoor to make sure it was still locked, he went to the living room and sat on the couch, held the remote in his hand but didn't turn on the TV.

He thought again about the little girl and Bradley, and the fact that Mrs. Williams had likely died in the very room he was sleeping in. And there was the night that he swore someone was walking across the floor, swore he saw movement, but when he had turned on the lights, no one was there. And, of course, there was the bed. For the life of him, he couldn't remember if he had made it.

He shook his head again and a nervous laugh escaped. He was being ridiculous, was letting a tragic and horrible story get in the way of reality. And reality pointed directly at bat man. He must know the story, must be looking for the money. Why else would he be sneaking around the house if not to dig up the basement floor and knock holes in the wall to see what was behind it? And why was he keeping tabs on Mike and Kayla, following them on their walks? He knew when Mike was out, must have discovered the backdoor was unlocked. It would be simple for him to walk in, search through the house, maybe turn off a light or two out of habit. And with access to the basement being outside, he could sneak in even when Mike was home. Even on stormy nights when he thought the rain and thunder might drown out the sounds he would make breaking the bricks of an old cellar wall loose.

The thing was, as much as the evidence suggested bat man was the culprit, Mike still couldn't wrap his head around it. It was entirely out of character for the guy.

Everything Mike knew about the town's resident superhero pointed to a harmless human being who only wanted to spread cheer in an often cheerless world. He was getting along in age, tall and lanky, though his stomach was inching its way over his utility belt. He waved at kids from the street corners and they waved back, sometimes stopping to have their picture taken. He handed out candy on Halloween, showed up at downtown events and festivals for more photo ops with the kids.

And he never said a word.

Mike sighed yet again and realized how ridiculous his life was becoming. He left the house, locking the front door as he went, and climbed back into his Jeep. The best course of action was to simply talk to bat man. Mike couldn't imagine there would be any danger in it, couldn't believe for a second that bat man was cut from the same cloth as Jeb Martin, that he would kill over money that probably didn't exist.

Mike had hoped to find the caped crusader standing on the corner at the stoplight, waving to passing cars, but no such luck. He circled through downtown several times to make sure, but there was no dark knight to be seen. Mike had no idea where the man lived. For all he knew, he was hanging upside down in a cave somewhere. Maybe Audrey knew. She knew the town inside and out. If anyone could tell him where to find the most recognizable figure in town, it would be her.

He drove back to the library and found Audrey sitting in one of the padded chairs, a book in her lap. She looked up and waved.

"Back for more bad news?" she asked as he took the chair across from her.

"Please tell me you didn't find something else."

Audrey grinned. "You're in luck. Nothing so far. So did you miss me so much you had to come back by, or are you just avoiding the house?"

"Neither. I was hoping you could tell me where I might find bat man."

A mischievous look crossed her face, the one she made when she was about to say something she thought was witty. "What about the bat cave? Did you check there?" she asked, her smile widening.

Mike closed his eyes a moment and took a long breath as Audrey continued.

"I think he hangs out in Gotham City a lot. Just check

in with the commissioner. He probably knows where to find him."

Mike waited as she giggled, then asked, "Are you done?"

Audrey pursed her lips and squinted as she thought. "I think so. Wait, one more. Do you need to borrow my bat signal? Will that help? It's in the back. I can run and get it."

Mike waited again for her giggling to subside.

"Amusing," he said.

"Yes, it is."

"So do you know where he lives or not? And if you don't give me a straight answer, so help me God, I will never speak to you again."

"Fine," Audrey said, an exaggerated frown on her face. She pulled her phone from her pocket and tapped on the screen. Mike waited patiently as she worked. When his phone dinged, Audrey looked up.

"There. That's the place."

Mike checked the message and found a link to an online map with a pin dropped to mark a location. He zoomed out and recognized the street. Only three blocks away from the house, close enough to easily drop in and dig for buried treasure.

"So, why do you want to know where bat man lives?"

Mike ignored the question. "Thanks for the info. Did anyone bring donuts today?"

"Yes."

"Sweet." Mike stood and headed for the breakroom.

When he glanced back, Audrey had returned her attention to the book in her lap.

Mike sat at the kitchen table, staring at the photographs and doing his best not to imagine the prone body of Horace Williams bleeding out on the floor.

When he had left the library, he had driven straight to bat man's house, but no one was home. No one answered his knock on the door, anyway. Who knew if bat man was actually inside or not? There was no vehicle in the drive, but then again, he had only ever seen the man walking.

He left the photos on the table and moved to the couch, where he stared at the blank TV screen. He considered calling Kayla, asking if it was okay to sleep in her mom's house until things got sorted out, but opted against it. She would still be on the road, and he preferred not to bother her with his problems. She had enough of her own.

A question popped into his head: How would Trevor react when Kayla confronted him? Had he grown and matured over the years, or was he still the same asshole Mike knew? Considering the circumstances, the latter was the safe bet. Mike was surprised to find he wasn't too worried Trevor would do something drastic. Even in high school, Mike had never known the guy to say a mean word or lift a finger to her.

And he had been fiercely protective of her, no matter what. He had dunked Mike's head in a toilet just for looking at her, although that may have been simply for his own sadistic pleasure.

But, there was the incident with Lance.

----

26 Years Earlier

They crept alongside the car, a midnight blue Trans Am bought with his parents' money. The back passenger side tire was already flat, just as Audrey had said it would be.

"Maybe we should leave well enough alone," Mike said, unsure why he was whispering.

"Screw that. He's probably got a spare he can put on. At the very least, I've caused him a minor inconvenience. But if we let the air out of all of them —"

She stopped when she heard voices in the distance, and held a finger to her lips.

"Is that him?" Mike whispered.

Audrey shot him a look and used her other hand to point at the finger still over her lips.

"Sorry," Mike whispered.

The voices drew closer, laughter mixed with profanities. Mike had a sinking feeling things were about to take a terrible turn.

Audrey motioned for Mike to follow and moved past him, on her hands and knees, to the rear of the car. As Mike caught up, she was already surveying their surroundings, formulating a plan.

The voices came closer.

"Hold up. I have to go whiz."

"Christ, Trevor. Hurry your ass up."

"Screw you," came the reply, already fading into the distance.

"Your boyfriend is a douche." It was the unmistakable voice of Lance. "By the way, I didn't say anything earlier, but you look super hot tonight."

"Thanks." That voice was Kayla and she sounded anything but sincere. Mike could feel the discomfort in it.

"You know, you ever get tired of Trevor, I think you and I would make a good pair."

Audrey and Mike looked at each other, wide-eyed, as they heard a slight, nervous laugh.

"What do you think?"

"I'm going to wait in the car. Trevor should be back any minute."

"Aw, come on. You can't tell me you haven't thought about it."

Mike couldn't quite believe what he was hearing, though he shouldn't have been surprised that the friendships among jerks like Trevor and Lance were only skin deep.

The sound of a door opening was followed by the shuffling of feet.

"Please knock it off."

The hair on the back of Mike's neck stood up as he and Audrey looked at each other again, neither knowing what to do.

"I would treat you way better than Trev. Damn, you are fine."

"Stop it."

Her words were more forceful, more urgent, and Mike knew Lance was taking things too far. Where was Trevor? Surely he would show up any minute and see what was going on.

Audrey moved to stand, but Mike grabbed her elbow and shook his head. She shot him a look as he held her in place.

"No, don't," he begged her.

The look on Audrey's face scorched Mike to his core. It was urgency mixed with disappointment and disgust at his inaction. He was hoping Trevor would return, that he and Audrey could stay hidden.

But that look. He couldn't bear it any longer.

"Stay here," he whispered and stood up.

The door to Trevor's car was still open. Inside, Kayla was barely illuminated by the dome light. Lance stood in the door, leaning in, his hands somewhere Mike couldn't see. Kayla was pushing against him, trying to slide away, further into the car.

"Stop it," she said. "Get your hands off me."

"Oh come on, you know you like it."

Mike had no idea what to do, but anger flared inside him. He strode forward and, without thinking, grabbed the open door and slammed it into Lance's backside.

"Hey, what the hell…"

Lance wheeled around, holding his elbow, and saw Mike standing there, in shock.

"Oh, you are dead."

Mike bolted as Lance lunged for him, sprinting back the way he had come. He expected a hand to clamp onto him, yank him to the ground where he would be pummeled, but it didn't happen. Instead, he heard a thud followed by a string of obscenities. He looked back to see Lance on the ground and Audrey with her leg sticking out from behind the car.

Lance rolled over, clutching his elbow, still cursing.

"Come on," Mike shouted to Audrey as she stood and ran toward him. Lance swiped at her leg as she ran past, but only found air.

"I'm gonna kill both of you," Lance shouted as they ran, Audrey holding the skirt of her dress up. When they reached Audrey's car, Mike risked a look back and saw Lance running toward them. Further back, Trevor was just returning.

It seemed like an eternity before they were in the car, engine started, and were moving.

Lance slapped the side and yelled something indecipherable as Audrey hit the gas and they sped away.

Mike shook the memory away, realizing his pulse had quickened. He took a few deep breaths and tossed the unused remote aside, then grabbed his keys and left.

After a quick stop at the grocery store for a loaf of bread, he circled through the neighborhood, checking for a vehicle at bat man's house. Still nothing. He contemplated knocking on the door again, but decided against it, returning to the house instead.

Dejected, he sat on the couch, having only killed half an hour. It was going to be a long evening and likely a longer night. Sleeping upstairs was out of the question, even if there was no such thing as ghosts. The couch was an option, as was Kayla's mom's house. In the end, it came down to respecting Kayla and her mom. He wouldn't use the house without asking. The problem was, he knew he couldn't bring himself to ask, was afraid he would look ridiculous in Kayla's eyes.

Resigning himself to a long night, he laid over on the couch and turned on the TV.

----

26 Years Earlier

Mike had been careful to avoid Lance the next day, but now that school had let out, all bets were off. As he and Audrey walked to her car, Lance popped up from behind it. He circled around and grabbed two fistfuls of Mike's shirt.

"You're dead meat, nerd."

"Get your hands off him," Audrey yelled, taking a step toward them. Mike held up a hand to stop her, not wanting her within Lance's reach. To his surprise, she stopped, her eyes asking him a silent question. He nodded, hoping she took it as confirmation to hold back.

"You like slamming doors on people, nerd? How about I slam your face?"

"I saw what you did," Mike managed to say, meeting Lance's eyes.

"You didn't see shit."

"I did. And if you don't let me go and leave both of us alone for good, I'm going to the cops."

Lance laughed. "The cops? You gonna run crying to the cops? Go ahead, I didn't do anything."

"You did," Mike said, trying to keep his voice steady. "I saw it."

Lance laughed again, but Mike saw there was something underneath it, a hint of doubt or nervousness. Something.

"You're seeing things, nerd. Besides, it's your word against mine. No one is going to believe anything you say."

"I saw it, too," Audrey said.

Lance whipped his head to the side and glared at her.

"And I'm sure Kayla will agree with us," Audrey continued. "Two witnesses and one victim would be awful hard for the police to ignore."

"The cops aren't going to do anything to me," Lance said, his lip curling into a sneer as he tightened his grip on Mike's shirt.

"What about Trevor?" Mike asked. "Does he know? I bet he wouldn't take the news well."

Lance barked out a short laugh, but Mike could plainly see a crack in his confidence.

"Like Trevor is going to believe a nerd that was eyeing his girl."

"He may not believe me," Mike said, "but I'm betting he'll believe if me, Audrey, and Kayla are all saying the same thing. Has she told him what happened yet? If not, I bet we can convince her."

Lance sneered again and drew in a sharp breath. Mike braced himself.

And then Lance let him go with a shove, turned and walked away.

"That guy is insane," Audrey said.

Mike nodded and let out a relieved breath. "Yeah, he is."

"Do you think he'll do anything?"

Mike shrugged. "I don't know. But I could see in his eyes that he was worried."

"I hope you're right," Audrey said.

Mike woke with a start. The living room was painted a muted gold with the low light of dusk as he realized he had drifted off to sleep. From the looks of it, he had been out a while.

A knock on the door caused him to jump.

"Jesus," he muttered, placing a hand over his pounding heart as he stood up and crossed the living room.

He pulled the door open and came face to face with bat man.

They stood still, looking at each other for a long moment as Mike's brain, still foggy from sleep, tried to process what was happening. Without a word, bat man held out a folded piece of paper. Mike eyed the paper before taking it, then watched in stunned silence as bat man turned and walked away, crossing the yard to the road, heading in the direction of his own home a few blocks away. His cape rippled in the dying light.

Mike opened his mouth to call out, realizing he was missing an opportunity to confront the guy about all the sneaking around, but stopped short. Bat man was already rounding the corner.

Mike surveyed the neighborhood and shook his head, wondering if anyone else was seeing the circus his life was becoming.

He closed the door and returned to the couch, where he unfolded the piece of paper. Written in large, shaky letters, were the words: BE CAREFUL. DON'T GO IN THE BASEMENT.

"What the hell?" he asked out loud. Was this supposed to be some sort of threat? Did bat man know that Mike had learned the legend of the money? Was this his way of telling Mike to stay out of the way?

Mike laughed out loud. The thought was ridiculous. There was no way an aging man in a superhero costume was hand-delivering written warnings about hidden money.

Tossing the paper onto the coffee table, Mike yawned and laid back down. He would confront bat man another day.

----

26 Years Earlier

Mike had been worried. He had kept a close eye on

Audrey and his head on a swivel, expecting further re-taliation from Lance.

It never came. Days later, after third period, as he closed his locker, Mike turned to see Lance walking by, his right eye swollen and bruised, a cut above his lip. Lance stared straight ahead as he passed.

That same afternoon, as school let out, Mike and Audrey were walking across the parking lot to her car when Trevor stepped out from behind a pickup truck, blocking their path. Mike noticed the scrapes on the knuckles of Trevor's right hand, wondering if his own face was about to add more.

"Leave us alone," Audrey said, defiant as always.

Trevor sneered at her. "How about you shut up and listen for a minute. I know what happened."

Audrey had opened her mouth to speak, not taking kindly to being told to shut up, but she stopped before any words came out.

"Kayla told me you helped her." Trevor was looking at Audrey as he spoke. "She told me what Lance did, told me someone slammed the door on him and took off. Said she didn't see who it was, but I'm pretty sure I did. That was your car tearing out of there, wasn't it?"

Audrey nodded, opened her mouth to speak again, but Trevor cut her off.

"You're in luck," he said, now focusing on Mike. "I don't know which one of you actually did it, but Lance was ready to kill both of you and I was more than happy to help until Kayla told me what he had done. The three of us here, we're all square. And you don't have to worry about Lance. I made sure he knows you two are off limits."

Mike wanted to breathe a sigh of relief, but he held it in.

"But if I catch you eyeing my girl again," Trevor continued, "all bets are off. Got it, nerd?"

Before Mike could reply, not that he was going to, Trevor strode off, bumping his shoulder against Mike's as he went. The guy just couldn't help but be an asshole.

Mike and Audrey looked at each other in something akin to disbelief.

"That went better than expected," Audrey finally said.

Mike woke again to his phone ringing. He fumbled for it before seeing Kayla's name on the caller ID and answering.

"Hi, I hope I'm not waking you."

"No, not at all," he lied. "How's the trip going? Are you there yet?"

"It's going fine. I'm about an hour outside the city."

"Are you stopped for the night?"

"Yes. Been settled into a hotel for a while and..." She trailed off for a moment. "I guess I just needed to hear a friendly voice."

"Well, you came to the right place. How are you holding up?"

She paused before answering. "Fine, I guess. The closer I get, the less I want to keep going."

"Understandable."

"So, how's your day been?"

Mike laughed. "You wouldn't believe me if I told you."

"Oh? Try me. I could use the distraction."

Mike told her about the audio reel, what he had learned from Audrey, and about bat man and the footprint in the basement, the hole in the wall, the legend of the hidden money, everything but the murder of Horace and the death of Martha.

"Wow. You weren't kidding. That's an interesting day."

"To say the least," Mike added.

They talked well into the night, about nothing in particular, at times bouncing a few thoughts about the hidden money and the house's history off each other. Around midnight, Mike heard a yawn on the other end of the line.

"I should probably go," Kayla said. "I'll probably get an early start in the morning."

"Sure," Mike said. "Yeah, I should probably try to get some sleep too. Big day of trying to solve mysteries and all."

He heard a small laugh and smiled.

"Good night," she said.

"Good night."

He sat the phone aside and stared at the walls, rehashing the day. There had been too many memories floating to the surface, too many things haunting him, both from the past and the present. Hopefully tomorrow wouldn't be more of the same. He went to the kitchen for a drink of water, checked that the backdoor was still locked, then returned to the couch and flicked the TV on.

It was going to be a long night.

Mike's back and right hip ached from spending the night on the couch. Sleep had mostly eluded him, but he had managed to doze off several times before being awakened by some noise or other. At times, he would stare at the floor, straining to hear any thuds coming from below, wondering if bat man was down there looking for Anson's hidden fortune.

He stretched and twisted and turned, trying to work away the stiffness as he peered out the front window. It was still early and the morning was overcast, dull and gray, a slight breeze stirring in the trees. The forecast was calling for rain off and on throughout the day, with the possibility of severe storms after dark. The clouds that were rolling in at the moment weren't menacing, but he knew the usual weather patterns. The severe stuff always seemed to come along after nightfall.

He gave up watching the world passing him by and ate breakfast, using the last of the eggs. As he was putting the dishes in the sink, his phone rang. When he checked the caller ID, he was surprised at what he saw.

"Hello Mr. Swanstrom."

"Mike, how are you?"

"Good, you?"

"Doing well. Did I catch you at a bad time?"

"Not at all," Mike said as he sat back down at the table. "What can I do for you?"

"We have a project we need help with. You know that custom piece you did for us a few years back? We've got another one we need. Can I send you the specs, let you review it, see if it's something you would be interested in?"

"Of course," Mike said. "I'd be happy to take a look."

"Excellent. I'm hitting send on the email now. I know it's the end of the week, but if you could let me know something close of business on Monday, I would appreciate it. I need to get the ball rolling sooner rather than later."

"No problem. I'll let you know something as soon as I can."

"Good deal. I'll wait to hear back."

Make stared at the phone a moment after hanging up, telling himself not to get too excited, it might be nothing, or it might be a small project that was next to nothing. Still, the fact that Mr. Swanstrom was emailing the specs rather than telling him over the phone seemed to indicate something larger. He slid his chair back and moved to the couch, grabbed his laptop and powered it on.

The email was already waiting in his inbox. When he opened it, he could tell right away the project was significant. On the surface, it looked exactly like what he needed to get back into the swing of things, to get money coming in instead of only going out, and to make another positive step toward getting his life back in order. He didn't want to get his hopes up, but it was certainly promising. And with money coming in, he could spring for another place, something less haunted by a morbid backstory.

The thought reminded him of Kayla's mother's house. Maybe he would go by and make sure everything was battened down, just in case the storms slated for the evening got bad. He could stop in at the library as well, then be back for lunch and spend the afternoon pouring through the project specs.

Satisfied with his plan, he took a shower, running the hot water out before stopping.

Wrapping a towel around his waist, he walked down the hall to the bedroom, feeling the hair on the back of his neck rise with each step. Stopping in the doorway, he stared at the bed. In his mind, he could see Martha lying there, taking her last breath.

And then getting up and gliding to the window to

watch a little boy named Bradley pedal by on his bike, stopping briefly to look her way.

Mike's skin crawled as he shook the thought away.

"Stop being such a baby," he mumbled and stepped into the room with as much confidence as he could muster.

After getting dressed, he left the light on and went back downstairs and out the front door.

The air outside was sticky and smelled of rain. By the time he drove the few blocks to the library, drops began falling, dotting the windshield. He jogged inside and found Audrey in her office.

"Sleep well last night?" she asked with a grin as he sat down across from her.

Mike sighed and rubbed his temple. "I know you think you're funny, but surely at this point in your life, someone has informed you otherwise."

She giggled. "Just because you have no sense of humor doesn't mean I'm not funny. Anyway, I'm glad to see you weren't carried off by ghosts. Oh, were you able to track down our local superhero?"

Mike leaned back in his chair. "No, but he got in touch with me."

"What do you mean?"

"He wasn't home when I went by, but he showed up later at my door. Handed me a note and left."

Audrey leaned forward and propped her elbows on her desk. "A note? What did it say?"

Mike could tell her interest was piqued, and he

couldn't resist taking advantage of the moment. He leaned forward, giving her his best serious stare. "You won't believe this, but it said—" He paused for dramatic effect. "—mind your own business."

Though he was kidding, Mike realized his joke was basically one and the same with the actual note. Bat man wanted him to stay out of the basement, effectively telling him to mind his own business.

"Fine," Audrey said. "Don't tell me. Like I want to know, anyway." She sneered at him as he laughed.

"Have you heard anything from the region?"

Her expression softened as she took a long, slow breath. "I wanted to talk to you about that."

Judging from the look in her eyes, the news wasn't good. Mike braced himself for the official word.

"I got it," she said.

Mike's mouth was already open, ready to offer condolences, when he processed what she had said. "Wait, what?"

"I got it," she repeated.

"That's great. Right?"

She nodded.

"Then why do you look like someone stole your bicycle?"

Her smile was sad as she looked at him, saying nothing.

"Ah," Mike said, understanding. "I get it. You think I'll be lost without you."

She offered only a slight nod.

"Look," he said, "I'll be fine. Things are looking up lately. I'll be good. Really."

"You come by here every day," she pointed out.

"I know, but it's fine. Really, it is. I mean, sure, I'll have to find someone else to annoy me, but that shouldn't be too hard because I'm easily annoyed."

"I'm sorry," she said, ignoring his attempt at humor.

"Don't apologize. If I get too bored, I'll just move as well. I mean, I *love* the place I'm in now, but I could part with it if I really had to."

She laughed at that one.

Outside, the rain picked up.

"When do you start?"

"Two weeks."

Mike's eyes widened. "Two weeks. Wow. They aren't wasting any time."

"I have to spend time with Anne before she retires, get up to speed on things, figure out what the heck I'm doing. I won't officially be the director for another six weeks. Until then, I'll be splitting my time between here and the main branch. Obviously, it will take time for us to get a place closer to the main branch, so in the meantime I'll be commuting. It won't be too bad, though. I still have to hire and train my replacement for this branch."

"Sounds like you've got some busy days ahead of you."

She nodded and grinned, finally letting her excitement slip through. "I can't wait. I have so many good ideas."

Mike picked at the seam on the leg of his jeans and

nodded. "I know. Just don't let all that power go to your head." A familiar feeling was welling up inside him and he quickly recognized it. It was the same way he had felt, all those years ago, sitting in the treehouse, worried what would happen to him if his friend moved away.

"I can't make any promises," she said.

He smiled and looked up at her. "I'm so proud of you. You're going to do great."

She stood and came around the desk, pulled him to his feet and threw her arms around his neck.

"Thank you," she said, her voice cracking.

Mike hugged her back, and when she finally pulled away, she wiped at her eyes.

"Now look what you've done."

"Geez," Mike said, grinning. "You're such a big baby."

"Don't tell Dave."

They made small talk a while longer, then Audrey walked with him to the door where they paused in the foyer, watching the rain fall.

"Looks like it'll be a quiet day," she said. "I doubt we get many visitors in this weather. Maybe I'll do some more research on the house."

Mike groaned. "If you find out about any more deaths, please keep them to yourself."

"Will do." Audrey elbowed him gently in the side. "You good?"

Mike nodded, resisting the urge to tell her about the potential project. He didn't want to get ahead of himself.

"Yeah. You?"

She nodded in return.

"Good."

"Hey, you never told me why you were wanting to talk to bat man?"

"Oh, that. I think he's been sneaking into my basement and digging for the lost gold of Anson Krebs. Gotta run."

He pushed his way through the door and into the rain before she could react.

Mike drove straight to Kayla's mom's house and pulled into the driveway. He grabbed the umbrella he kept behind the seat and popped it open as he got out. Circling the house, he made sure the doors were locked and all the windows were down. There was no lawn furniture or other items that would be blown about if the storms turned severe, and the door to the shed was still padlocked. All was well.

Climbing back in the Jeep, he shook the water from the umbrella and tossed it in the back. Before starting the engine, he stared at the house and realized that, if Kayla did decide to rent the place to him, living there might not be any better than his current residence, with the exception of the town superhero digging for treasure in the basement. At the end of the day, he would still be occupying space where someone had died, and that might be hard to ignore.

He ate lunch at Jackson's Café, just beating the lunch crowd, and found himself thinking back to his last meal there, Kayla sitting across from him. He wondered how her drive was going. Hopefully, her talk with Trevor would be just that, a talk. He considered calling her, suggesting she take a friend with her, just to be safe. He still didn't think Trevor would hurt her physically, but maybe he was being naive.

After paying the check, he sat in his Jeep, holding his phone in his hand, telling himself he should call, just to say hello and wish her luck then possibly throw in the idea of taking a friend. Surely she wouldn't walk into a dangerous situation, but then again, she might be blind to it after all these years.

He dialed and held the phone to his ear, waiting as the number of rings mounted until her voicemail greeting came on. With a long sigh, he hung up and tossed the phone onto the passenger seat, then started the engine.

Back at the house, he spent the rest of the afternoon pouring over the project proposal. The more he read, the more he had alternated between excited and nervous. The project was big, easily four months of work. Diving back in on that kind of scale was scary, but still he was optimistic. He put the laptop aside and yawned, deciding it would be best to take a break, then come back with a refreshed mind and give it one last review before committing.

Outside the living room window, the sky was gray and gloomy, unchanged from that morning. A light rain was falling, barely audible inside the house. He stood and stretched, trying to shake some life back into his limbs after sitting and staring at the screen for so long, and decided it would do him good to get out again for a bit.

The parking lot of the grocery store was deserted when Mike pulled in. The rain was picking up as he walked briskly to the front doors, hopping over a puddle to keep his shoes somewhat dry. When the automatic doors slid open, he could see Monotone Checkout Girl at the only open register, wiping down the conveyor. She glanced up, blank expression as usual, then returned to her task.

Overhead, a familiar song played, though he couldn't name the title or the artist. He walked slowly through the aisles, browsing as he went, hoping something might catch his eye that would add variety to his diet. Since the divorce, he had kept his meal plan simple, if you could call it a plan at all. Maybe he should shake things up a bit.

By the time he reached the dairy section in the back corner, nothing had jumped out at him. It would be business as usual for a while longer, but that was fine. He grabbed a carton of eggs, flipped it open to make sure none were busted, then slowly ambled his way to the front.

Monotone Checkout Girl was adding plastic bags to the holder when he walked up.

"Hey, Mr. Ellerton," she said.

"Stop calling me that. It makes me sound old."

"Sure thing, Mr. Ellerton."

She hit the button on the conveyor and they watched the eggs slowly make their way forward.

"Will this be all?"

"Still no matsutake, so yeah."

She fixed him with her usual blank stare as she reached over and hit the total button on the register without taking her eyes off him.

"Impressive," Mike said, handing over his credit card.

"You eat a lot of eggs."

Mike nodded and waited for her to hand his card back. "How's class?"

"Almost over. I'm never taking summer courses again."

"Well, I think it shows great initiative that you would get a head start on college like that. You're going to be a productive member of society one of these days. I bet you'll be wearing pantsuits before long."

"Ew, no I won't, shut up."

Mike laughed and swore he saw her lips twitch, fighting off a grin. He grabbed his eggs and started for the door, then called back over his shoulder. "Be careful tonight. Storms are coming."

He jogged to his Jeep, taking care not to jostle the eggs too much. Thunder rumbled somewhere in the distance as he started the engine and pulled out of the lot. Rather than going straight back home, he circled through town, passing by Kayla's mom's once more. Nothing had changed from earlier, of course, but it was a good excuse to kill a few extra minutes.

On his way back through town, he noticed more

cruisers than usual at the police station. Probably adding a few extra shifts to deal with any issues the storms might bring.

Minutes later, as he pulled back into the driveway, the rain eased to a light sprinkle. He took his time getting out and going inside, looking toward the back corner of the yard and beyond to the courthouse as he did so. No caped figures lurked about that he could see.

Inside, he placed the eggs in the refrigerator and tossed the grocery bag in the trash. He made a sandwich as his stomach growled, wishing he had found something new to eat after all. Before digging in, he grabbed his laptop and sat it beside his dinner on the kitchen table, then alternated between eating and typing. By the time the sandwich was gone, he had finished the email to Mr. Swanstrom saying he wanted the project. Instead of hitting send, he saved it in the drafts folder. Though he had decided to take on the work, he still worried it was too much too soon. Leaving the email unsent until Monday would give him time to prepare mentally to move from doing nothing to working all out for the next few months.

Stifling a yawn, he slid his chair back from the table and went upstairs, the stairwell groaning beneath him with each step. He brushed his teeth, washed his face in the sink, then returned to the living room and plopped down on the couch.

He flipped the TV on as he settled back into the cushions, leaving the volume low, barely audible. There was no need to discern what was being said, he just wanted a faint background noise to help lull him to sleep. Not that he really needed the help. The rain had started up again and, on top of that, he was tired. Most likely, he would be asleep in no time.

As daylight faded and the room darkened, he realized he hadn't turned on the overhead light, but he opted to leave it off. He was already comfortable and getting up seemed too big a chore.

On the screen, the DA was making her case to the jury. He blinked a few times, nice and slow, and each time his eyelids grew heavier and were harder to raise until finally, he gave in. The insides of his eyelids pulsed from the light of the TV that forced its way through, but even that began to fade.

Mike gasped and opened his eyes, his heart thudding in his chest. The surrounding room was lit only by the blue glow of the TV, which had moved on from its court-room drama to an old sitcom rerun.

He shook his head to clear it, unsure why his pulse was racing. Had something awakened him? Had he been dreaming? If so, he couldn't remember a single shred of it.

Around him, shadows danced in every corner of the room, and he wished he had turned on the overhead light after all. He should have known better. It wasn't his first rodeo in the house.

He moved to stand up, but froze when the stairs

behind him groaned, as though under the weight of someone... or something. He spun his head around, his skin crawling as he stared at the stairs. The lower portion was lit by the TV, but further up was pitch black. Several moments passed before he tore his gaze away from the darkness and bolted for the light switch.

There was nothing there. No ghosts, no superheroes, nothing. He took a few deep breaths to slow his heart rate.

"You're such an idiot," he said out loud. "Stop freaking yourself out."

Shaking his head in disgust, he went back to the couch. He turned the volume up on the TV, hoping the extra sound would make the house feel less foreboding.

It didn't.

The hair on the back of his neck stood on end as he couldn't stop picturing the stairs behind him.

They creaked again, and he almost jumped out of his skin. He spun, but once more, they were empty.

He took a deep breath as he chastised himself. No ghosts were floating around the house, turning off lights and causing the floorboards to creak. Everything had an explanation, one that was firmly rooted in reality. Old houses creaked: that was a fact. And there was the back-door that had been unlocked until recently. And there was a guy in a superhero costume snooping around. It only made sense he had discovered the unlocked door, had come in for a look when Mike was out and, probably out of habit, had shut off a light or two. That covered all the bases, plain and simple. It wasn't the ghost of Martha flipping the switches, and it wasn't the ghost of Anson Krebs knocking around in the basement, looking for his money. It was one man: a living, breathing man. And Mike planned to put an end to it tomorrow, for his own sanity.

Settling back in on the couch, he drifted to sleep as lightning flashed and thunder rumbled in the distance.

A crash woke Mike and he bolted upright. The house was dark, the TV off. Rain was pouring down outside, the wind howling and splattering drops against the windows. Mike stood and fumbled his way to the light switch and flipped it, but nothing happened. He glanced out the window and, despite the downpour, could see that the neighborhood was dark.

He stumbled back to the couch to find his phone. When the screen lit up, there were three notifications. The first was a low battery warning. The other two were a missed call and a text message. Both were from Audrey.

Call me, the text read. *I found something else.*

"Ah geez," Mike mumbled, hoping the body count hadn't risen.

The time was just after 11. Not too late to give her a call. It was Friday, after all; she was probably still up. Especially with the storm in full force outside. He switched on the flashlight app and went into the kitchen to find the actual flashlight, which was on the counter where he had left it. He turned it on, then closed the flashlight app on his phone to conserve what little battery remained, and sat down at the table.

If he was lucky, he could talk Audrey into letting him come over for a while. Even though he knew there was nothing supernatural going on in the house, he still wasn't thrilled at the prospect of being alone in the dark all night with the wind howling and lightning creating a strobe effect that did nothing to ease the creepiness.

He hit the call button as the low battery warning flashed again. Audrey picked up on the third ring.

"Make it quick," Mike said, "I'm almost out of battery. Power's out as well. And if you found another body, I prefer not to know."

"It's not another body," Audrey said. "It's something else. I thought you were joking earlier about bat man digging in your basement, until I stumbled across something. There was a trespassing report filed on the property about a month or so before you moved in. You're not going to believe —"

The phone went dead. Mike pulled it from his ear and hit the power button, but the screen stayed dark.

"Great."

Though she was cut off, Mike was sure Audrey was

about to confirm what he suspected. Bat man had been caught trespassing before, and now he was back up to his old tricks.

Just as he was about to stand up, Mike heard a thump. He froze, telling himself it was just distant thunder or maybe a limb from one of the trees coming down in the wind. A second thump came a moment later. This time, he was sure it came from below.

"All right," he said out loud, "that's it." He'd had enough. He wasn't going to wait to track bat man down, he was going to put an end to this nonsense right now.

Careful not to scrape the chair on the floor, he stood and walked gingerly to the backdoor, not wanting to give any warning that he was on the move.

Easing the door open, he stepped out into the pouring rain. Lighting flashed, illuminating the cellar door that stood wide open. In the few seconds it took to reach it, Mike was already soaked. As he peered down the steps, a dim light emanated from inside.

Placing his foot on the first step, he paused and wondered if he should wait after all, but decided against it. He moved slowly, the rain beating at his back until he was halfway down. As he neared the bottom, the source of the light came into view. A flashlight sat on the ground off to his left, by the pile of loose bricks. Its beam shone slightly up at the brick wall only a few feet away, and the back of a pair of legs, visible from the knees down, stood beside it. As expected, the legs wore large black boots.

Mike took another step down, revealing more of the legs. Then another.

Something was off, but he was having trouble processing it.

He took another step and another until he was on the dirt floor of the basement, where he could see the back of the figure in its entirety.

Mike didn't know who it was, but he knew for sure it wasn't bat man. The build was too wide, too sturdy and large. There was no cape, just dark work pants and a raincoat. The man, whoever he was, held a sledgehammer that he rammed into a brick, knocking it loose.

Mike had a bad, bad feeling. His heart climbed into his throat and he stepped back, looking to retreat up the stairs, but his foot missed the bottom step and he fell back, sitting down hard on the next step up.

The man at the wall stopped, stood still for a long moment, then slowly turned. Mike almost fainted.

The man's face was all too familiar; it was the spitting image of the mugshot Audrey had shown him of the man who had killed Horace Williams, the man who had been put to death in prison.

It only took Mike a split second to realize he was in trouble as the man dropped the sledgehammer and strode toward him. Mike scrambled to his feet and bolted up the stairs, feeling the brush of something against his ankle as he climbed. Exiting the cellar, he looked back and saw the man on the stairs only feet behind him.

Mike turned and ran for all he was worth. As he rounded the corner of the house, his foot slipped in the mud, sending him crashing down on his hip and elbow in a puddle of murky water. He glanced back as the dark outline of the man strode around the corner, walking with a grim purpose like a killer in a horror movie. He hesitated when he saw Mike on the ground.

Lightning flashed, illuminating the man's face. In that brief moment, Mike could see bad things in the man's eyes.

The man darted forward and Mike turned, clawing his way to his feet to run, but was hit from behind and tackled to the ground. Water splashed, carrying mud and debris with it. The man crawled onto Mike's back, placed a large hand on Mike's head, and began pushing his face toward the water. Mike struggled, pushed back with all his strength, managed to hold his own for a second before slowly losing the battle. As his nose touched the muddy water, the memory of the homecoming dance flashed through his mind and he could see Trevor pushing his face toward the bowl. Mike had the sickening realization that this time around, his assailant intended to do more than just humiliate him: he intended to drown him. With every bit of strength Mike could muster, he twisted to the side, rolled his hips and brought his elbow up and back. He connected with the man's ribs, heard him grunt as he fell to the side. Mike squirmed to his hands and knees, but the man was already up. His foot connected with Mike's ribs, knocking Mike onto his back. Clutching his side, Mike scrambled back to his hands and knees again as the man stalked around, swung his large boot at Mike's face. Mike ducked to the side as water splashed. The man kicked again, only this time he aimed for the ground, kicking water and mud into Mike's eyes. Mike rubbed frantically, trying to clear his vision as he stood. Something smashed into his stomach, whether it was the man's foot or fist, Mike couldn't tell. He doubled over and dropped to his knees, gasping for air and still wiping at his eyes. As he managed to clear away enough of the muddy water to open them, he saw the blurry outline of the man walking away, disappearing around the corner of the house.

Mike continued wiping at his eyes until his vision was clear, then struggled to his feet. He was still catching his breath from the shot he had taken to the stomach when the man reappeared, striding around the corner with that same relentless walk. In his right hand was the sledgehammer. As Mike panicked, movement caught his eye over the man's shoulder. In the distance, through a break in the bushes, bat man stepped into view around the corner of the courthouse, reached into his utility belt and pulled out a small rectangle, then disappeared back into the shadows.

Mike realized the rectangle was a phone and won-dered if bat man was calling the police — lot of good it would do, though. With a sledgehammer wielding night-mare come to life and closing in on him, Mike knew the officer's main job tonight would be identifying his body.

Even though the station was only a mile away, it was too far for them to save him.

As the man neared, he suddenly charged, wielding the hammer like a baseball bat, and swung for the fences. Mike fell to his hands and knees, the hammer passing where his head had been. Even in the pouring rain, he heard it whoosh by.

The man had swung with such force that he stumbled, his momentum and the weight of the hammer carried him past Mike. Mike splashed his way to his feet, turned around to see the man had already recovered his balance. He brought the handle of the hammer up, catching Mike under his chin, then pulled back and popped him again in the nose.

Mike fell back, sending muddy water flying around him. Pain shot through his chin and nose and flashed bright in his vision. He tried to get up, but his arms and legs were sluggish, not doing what he wanted them to do.

The man stepped forward and stood over Mike as lightning flashed and thunder cracked. Mike swore he heard the man cursing as he raised the hammer over his head.

"No! Stop!"

The man paused, turned to look at the figure that had appeared behind him. It took Mike a moment to process what was happening. Had bat man come to help? No, the voice was too high, and the last Mike had seen him, he had ducked out of sight at the courthouse. The figure that Mike and the man both stared at now was someone else. Someone entirely unexpected.

It was Kayla.

The man lowered the hammer, turned and walked toward her.

Mike's heart sank, but he gathered himself enough to yell.

"Run!"

The man looked back at Mike, his face illuminated in a flash of lightning. He now wore a grin that scared Mike to death.

He turned away and continued on, raising the hammer as he neared Kayla. She stumbled back, her hands held out in a desperate attempt to shield herself.

Mike could see what was about to happen, but from where he lay in the muddy water, he was too far away to do anything about it. A scream rose in him, building somewhere down deep and rushing up. It died in his throat as something ran by, moving fast. Mike only caught a sense of the figure, but knew what it was.

Bat man shot past him, grabbed the head of the hammer in both hands from behind the man and held on, keeping it from coming down on Kayla. The man looked over his shoulder, then spun and stepped to the side, yanked hard on the hammer, pulling bat man forward and sending him crashing into Kayla. They went down in a heap. Bat man rolled over as the man stood still, towering before them, the hammer hanging at his side. Mike could only assume the man was trying to process what he was seeing: a guy in a costume, appearing out of nowhere. Mike himself was having trouble. The night had certainly taken a strange turn.

Mike shook his head to clear it and saw his chance. Rage shot through him and his adrenaline kicked in. He pushed his way to his feet, the pain in his nose still blurring his vision.

Slowly, the hammer began to raise.

Mike staggered forward as the hammer gained altitude, bat man and Kayla lying prone before it.

Mike closed the gap. Before the hammer could start its descent, Mike grabbed it with both hands, just as bat man had done, but he wasn't going to give the man a chance to shake him loose. He pulled back with everything he had, breaking the hammer free. Mike stumbled backward, losing his balance and releasing his grip as he sat down hard in the mud, the hammer landing at his feet. The man spun, strode toward him. Mike leaned forward to grab the hammer, but the man brought his boot up, kicked Mike in the chest and knocked him flat on his back. Mike heard a curse but couldn't see the man's face in the dark and the pounding rain. He could, however, see him scoop up the hammer and raise it over his head.

Mike relaxed as blue light flashed in the distance. The cavalry was coming, though it was far too late for him. He took comfort in the fact that Kayla would be okay. Bat man, too. The cops were coming fast. After the man was finished with him, there would be no time to hurt anyone else. Or so Mike hoped.

A dark outline appeared behind the man, topped by pointed ears. Gloved hands grabbed the head of the hammer again as Mike watched in awe. Bat man immediately kicked the back of the man's leg, causing him to buckle to a knee, releasing the hammer as he went. Bat man, now in control of the hammer, jabbed the head of the sledge into the back of the man's skull, sending him forward onto Mike's feet, face down in the mud, unmoving.

Mike looked up through the rain at the caped crusader, standing over them both like the superhero he was. Their eyes met and Mike smiled, started to laugh. Bat man looked behind him, the flashing blue lights now close and bright. He dropped the hammer and ran. Moments later, the first police cruiser slid to a stop on the road.

Mike laid his head back in the shallow water and closed his eyes, felt the rain on his face and the adrenaline still pumping through his veins. When he opened them, Kayla was at his side, kneeling in the mud.

"Are you okay?" she yelled over the pounding rain.

"What are you doing here?" Mike asked, smiling.

Kayla smiled back at him, her hair plastered to her head, water running down her beautiful face.

"I remembered you."

"What?" Mike asked. He was confused. Of course she remembered him. She had only been gone a short time.

"I remembered you," she said again, then added, "from high school. The homecoming dance. I remember."

More cars pulled up.

"Are you okay?" A cop yelled as he approached, his hand on his gun. It was Mike's old classmate.

"Fine," Mike yelled back. "This guy on my feet tried to kill us."

The cop rolled the man over, said something into his radio, then pulled out a pair of handcuffs.

Mike turned his attention back to Kayla as lightning flashed.

She pushed aside the wet hair plastered to her face. "It was you, wasn't it? You were the one who helped me that night. The night of the homecoming dance. I came to tell you I remembered."

"I don't understand," Mike said. "You were almost home last night, how did you —"

"I turned around," she interrupted. "I realized there was no point in going back. I called Trevor early this morning and told him I knew." A smile spread across her face as she shrugged. "And then I drove straight here."

Mike struggled to his knees, put his arms around her waist and pulled her close. When he kissed her, the sweet taste of her lip gloss mixed with mud and rain. It was the best taste he had ever experienced.

Around them, first responders had gathered. An ambulance was pulling up, along with every cop in the town. Rain continued to pour from the sky and Mike continued to kiss her as a circle formed around them.

Three Weeks Later

On his way to the library, Mike found him in the usual spot, standing on the corner of Main, waving at cars as they passed. He stopped and rolled down his window. As bat man walked over, they nodded to each other in greeting. Mike picked up the box from the passenger seat and opened it, held it out. Bat man studied the contents a moment before reaching in and pulling out a donut. He sniffed it, then took a bite. They nodded again, and bat man returned to the sidewalk, munching on the donut as he resumed waving.

Mike sat the box of donuts on the breakroom table, then found Audrey at her desk.

"Did you see this?" she asked, holding up the local newspaper.

Mike nodded as he took a seat. He had seen the headline, but hadn't bothered reading the story. Likely, he already knew more details than the article contained, thanks to his old classmate, Officer Reynolds, who had kept him informed during the investigation. As the details emerged, it had all made sense.

The man in the basement was Victor Reese, the great-grandson and spitting image of Jeb Martin, murderer of Horace Williams. The story of his great-grandfather's demise had been told in the family periodically, and Victor, in and out of trouble with authorities, decided one day he'd had enough. Enough petty theft and small-time drug dealing just to scrape by. One big score was all he needed to turn things around, head to Mexico and sit on the beach drinking margaritas and watching the pretty girls playing in the waves. The only problem was, he didn't have a plan until late one night, lying in the drunk tank of a small-town police department while cursing his family lineage, which he blamed for his predicament.

What if, he thought.

What if the story was true? What if there really was gold, smuggled back from the war, still hidden away? He was always hearing about gold prices reaching all-time highs. If it was there, what would it be worth? Only one way to find out.

When he started, the house had been empty, making things easy. So easy, in fact, that he grew complacent and got caught sneaking through the yard. After a trespassing charge, he laid low a while before resuming his search.

It wasn't long until someone moved in, throwing a wrench in his plans. It would slow things down, but he wasn't going to let it stop him. He just had to be extra careful, sneak in at night, not make noise.

He dug hole after hole hoping to get lucky, but the more he dug, the more he kept coming up empty. Not only that, but he grew increasingly agitated. Patience was never his strong suit. And then it hit him. The brick wall looked older, out of place. Maybe that was the key. He had begun working on it one night until hearing movement overhead. He had returned on a stormy night, hoping the rain and thunder would mask his sounds. But then, the guy renting the place had walked in.

Audrey had figured it all out, having found the trespassing report and tracing Victor Reese all the way back to Jeb Martin. Earlier that day, she had thought Mike was joking about bat man digging in the basement, but when she realized he wasn't, and that it was likely Reese, she grew worried. She called Mike but was cut short by his phone going dead. She quickly grew worried, jumped in her car, and drove through the storm. When she saw blue lights as she approached the house, she almost fainted.

"I still can't believe no one was seriously hurt," she said. "Or killed. Thank goodness our local superhero was there to save the day."

Mike nodded. Looking back, he could only assume bat man had seen Victor sneaking around the house one night while he was out doing whatever he was doing. Bat man had then kept an eye on Victor and a close watch on Mike and Kayla, had even tried warning Mike with a hand-delivered note that Mike had mistaken for a threat. And then, when all of their paths had crossed, he leapt into action, no doubt surprising himself as much as he surprised everyone else. And only four people knew about it. Five, if you counted bat man himself.

"I still don't see why you didn't tell the police," Audrey said.

Mike shrugged. "The way he ran off, I just assumed he wanted nothing to do with any of the aftermath. Can't say I blame him."

"Still, it would have been great if it was in the papers. The whole town should know. Did he ever tell you what he was doing there?"

"Maybe you haven't noticed, but he isn't much for words. And besides, I never asked."

"Why not?"

"I don't know. I guess some things are just better left to the imagination."

Audrey grinned. "Yeah, I guess so. Of course, I could have saved all of you the trouble if you had just charged your phone."

36 Years Earlier

"So it's really happening?"

Audrey nodded, the book in her lap forgotten.

"I'm really sorry," Mike said.

Outside the treehouse, evening was falling. The first sounds of crickets were beginning as leaves rustled around them.

"Are you going to move away?" he asked.

Mike knew very little about people and even less about girls, but when Audrey looked at him, he knew what he was seeing in her eyes. She was sad and afraid, which in turn made him scared. He didn't want to lose his best friend.

"I don't know. I don't even know which one is leaving and which one is staying."

Mike pulled at a loose thread on the cuff of his jeans. "Who do you want to stay with?"

Audrey shrugged. "I don't know. I guess my mom."

Mike would have made the same choice in her shoes, knowing what he knew. Her dad had a tendency to drink. A lot. He never hurt Audrey or her mom as far as he knew, but Mike had seen movies about dads that drank in excess and it always ended the same. Maybe Mike was letting his imagination get carried away — maybe Audrey's dad simply drank to forget — but better safe than sorry. After all, in all those movies, the mom never beat anyone up. It seemed like the sure bet.

"Do you think she will still live here?" he asked.

Another shrug.

"I sure hope she does," he added.

He wanted to say more, to let Audrey know how much he would miss her if she left, how he would probably cry if that happened. He hated being such a big baby, but sometimes he couldn't help it. She was his best friend, though he had never told her that. Girls had cooties, after all. He didn't want the guys at school to think he was a weirdo.

Still, she was.

The string on his jean cuff broke loose and he held it up and looked at it, then tossed it aside.

"If I have to leave," Audrey whispered, staring at the book in her lap, "do you promise we'll stay friends?"

Mike nodded.

Somewhere higher in the tree, a cicada sounded.

"I don't want to leave," she said. The words came out choked as she began crying.

Mike had no idea what to do or say, so he searched his cuffs for another loose thread to pull but found nothing.

"We'll still see each other at school," he finally said. "We can play at recess and everything. Maybe we'll be in the same class again next year."

Audrey wiped at her eyes, dragging her entire forearm across them as she sniffled. "What if I have to move to another school?"

That would never happen, Mike thought, desperately trying to convince himself. There was no way her parents would take her away from her school, her friends, her bedroom, this treehouse. All the things she knew and had ever known. There was just no way. They couldn't do that to her. Couldn't do that to him.

They leaned back against the wall and said nothing. Audrey reached over and took his hand and they sat there, unmoving as the evening grew darker and darker, until Audrey's mom called for her from the backdoor.

Two Months Later

Dave pulled the door of the moving truck down and latched it, then turned back to the house and put his hands on his hips.

"I guess that's it."

"I guess so," Audrey said, hooking her arm in his.

They stared at the house for a long moment as Mike stood quietly by, not wanting to interrupt.

Dave sighed and kissed Audrey on the forehead, then turned to Mike.

"Thanks for the help."

Mike nodded and looked away, trying to find something to focus on. He landed on a single lily in the flower bed.

"I'll make sure we didn't miss anything and lock up," Dave said to Audrey, then went inside.

"You okay?" Audrey asked Mike, walking to him.

He nodded again, met her eye for an instant. He didn't want to get emotional, didn't want to put a damper on the day. It was a big step forward for her and he was happy for his friend. All the sadness was for himself.

"Have you decided what you're going to do?"

Mike shook his head.

She wrapped her arms around his neck and he hugged her back.

"So, you start flying solo next week?" he managed to say as they let go.

Audrey nodded and smiled. "You may not believe this, but I'm truly nervous for the first time. I mean, it's the entire region. What if I screw it up?"

"You? Screw something up? No way. You'll be great at it, just like you are at everything else. It's so annoying."

She slapped him on the arm as they laughed. The front door opened and Dave reappeared, checking the lock before pulling it shut.

"Ready?" he asked.

"Ready," Audrey replied.

"Don't be a stranger," he said to Mike, picking him up in a bear hug that squeezed all the air out of Mike's lungs. He dropped him and headed around the truck toward the driver's seat.

"You heard him," Audrey said. "Don't be a stranger."

"I won't." Mike walked her to the passenger door, wondering what he would do without her close by. Not only had he grown accustomed to their daily visits, but it was Audrey that had kept him from drowning during the worst of the flood. He wasn't sure where he would be without her. Just as other parts of his life were coming together and things were looking up, being separated from her, even if the distance wasn't great, sucked.

He reached for the door handle but paused. "You're the best person I know."

She smiled, her eyes growing watery. "Yeah, I am pretty remarkable."

He pulled the door open and waited for her to climb in.

"Fingers and toes," he said.

"All clear."

He shut the door and watched them drive away.

Later that evening, the downstairs lights were still on when Mike pulled into the driveway. As he climbed out of the Jeep, he glanced toward the back corner of the house, then on to the courthouse where the silhouette of a man wearing a cape stood. A hand raised for a moment, then dropped. Mike returned the gesture and went inside.

Mike left the living room light on and locked the front door behind him as he left. He picked up the two pizzas he had called in earlier, placing them on the passenger seat as he inhaled. The smell made his stomach growl. When he pulled in behind Kayla's SUV, she was already waiting on the porch.

The living room of her mother's house was no longer empty. New furniture covered the indentions in the carpet, and the walls were beginning to fill with decorations that made the place feel alive again.

A new kitchen table, small with only two chairs, sat in the middle of the linoleum, but they opted for the couch instead. Kayla grabbed two paper plates from the cabinet and two bottles of water from the refrigerator and piled them alongside the pizza on the coffee table.

She was quiet, much more so than usual. Mike gave her time to come around before finally breaking the silence.

"Nervous?"

She attempted a smile, but it barely landed. "A little."

Mike couldn't blame her for being apprehensive. She had been dreading the trip back to Indianapolis for weeks, but it had to be done. While there, she would finalize her divorce, pack up and ship her belongings, and make a clean break from her old life. Though he felt for her, Mike was also jealous; she was making strides forward much quicker than he had.

Not long after that stormy night in the side yard, a teaching position had opened up at the elementary school. Though Kayla was still reeling from the sudden turn her life had taken, unsure where she would go and what she would do, she applied. Two weeks later, she was offered the position. It didn't take long for her to decide she would resign from her job in Indy. The next day, she accepted the position and went shopping for furniture.

"You know you can call any time."

She nodded. "I know."

Mike placed his hand on hers for a brief moment, hoping to reassure her but not overstep any bounds. Their kiss in the downpour, kneeling in the mud with a circle of emergency personnel around them, had not only been their first, but had so far been the only one. Mike knew Audrey was right; he had to let Kayla work her way through the divorce on her own schedule. Anything more right now would be foolish. It wouldn't be easy, but he would wait.

As they finished the pizza, Kayla slowly relaxed and returned to some semblance of her usual self. They discussed the upcoming school year and how much she was looking forward to meeting the students and getting back to work. It would be a welcomed constant in an uncertain world.

Around ten, Mike stood and took the empty pizza box to the trash, no longer just a bag hanging on the pantry door but a proper can. Kayla followed him into the kitchen and ran her finger along the new table.

"You sure you're all right?" he asked.

"Of course," she lied. "It's just six days. I'll get through it."

She walked him out. The night air was warm and still, the neighborhood quiet except for the chirping of crickets.

"Thanks for taking me to the airport in the morning. Sorry it's going to be so early."

"No worries," Mike said as he stepped off the porch. "I'll pick you up at six sharp." He walked a few paces toward the driveway before stopping and facing her. "If you have trouble sleeping, feel free to call."

"Sure," she said, grinning. "Is that more for you than me?"

"Maybe," Mike said. He didn't like to admit it, but the house still kept him up some nights. And there was the fact Kayla would be facing Trevor for the first time in months. That alone made him nervous.

He moved to turn away, but stopped once more. "Hey, what do you remember about the homecoming dance? I mean during, not what happened after."

Her eyes stared off into the night for several beats before she answered. "Not much really. Just that I never got to dance. That wasn't something Trevor liked to do."

Mike was glad she still didn't remember the incident in the lobby, as he fled with his wet hair, and how she had tried to help him up. Maybe she would one day, but he was fine if it never happened. It wasn't his best moment.

An idea struck. He held up a finger, hurried to his Jeep and opened the door. He turned the key one click and the radio lit up. It took a moment to find a station playing a good song, but once he found it, he walked back to Kayla, the notes carrying from the Jeep to the porch.

"May I have this dance?" he asked, holding out his hand.

A bashful smile spread across Kayla's face as she looked down at her feet.

"I'd like that."

She took his hand and they moved together onto the grass, to the edge of the porch light's halo, and danced.

MORE BOOK FROM KEVIN JOHNSON

The Hill

The Hill II

Bridging the Gap

For more information, visit kevinjohnsonwriter.com.